The Tiger

and

Other Tales

Jack Foley

© 2016 by Jack Foley
Book design © 2016 by Sagging Meniscus Press

All Rights Reserved.

Printed in the United States of America.
Set in Mrs. Eaves XL with LaTeX.

ISBN: 978-1-944697-13-6 (paperback)
ISBN: 978-1-944697-14-3 (ebook)
Library of Congress Control Number: 2016944019

Sagging Meniscus Press
web: http://www.saggingmeniscus.com/
email: info@saggingmeniscus.com

For Adelle in memoriam.

"Il y'a longtemps que je t'aime
Jamais je ne t'oublierai"

My mother thought it might do me good to write down my day-to-day experiences and emotions. What she didn't know was that I thought my life was terribly boring, and the last thing I wanted to do was to write about myself. Instead, I began to write about people other than me and things that never really happened. And thus began my life-long passion for writing fiction. So from the very beginning, fiction for me was less of an autobiographical manifestation than a transcendental journey into other lives, other possibilities.... Literature has to take us beyond. If it cannot take us there, it is not good literature.

—Elif Shafak, "The Politics of Fiction"

The universe is one being. Everything and everyone is interconnected through an invisible web of stories. Whether we are aware of it or not, we are all in a silent conversation. Do no harm. Practice compassion.

—Elif Shafak, *The Forty Rules of Love*

Is there a better medicine than poetry? I don't know of it.

—Heathcote Williams

To stress "the strangeness and the power of poetry" as opposed to its self-serving gregariousness or its technocratic sycophancy....

—Geoffrey Hill

Author's Note

I have been reading Evelyn Barish's attack biography of that scoundrel, Paul de Man, with whom I studied in the 1960s. Fascinating. What scrapes he got himself into. He embezzled funds from a publishing house he was involved in, lied his way into Harvard, was technically a bigamist, sheltered Jews, wrote anti-Semitic articles for a newspaper published by his uncle Henri de Man, who was a Belgian collaborationist. His past was constantly almost catching up with him. Yet the sheer brilliance of his mind impressed everyone who ever came across him—me included. It was a wonderful thing to watch him unfold a poem, a piece of writing. He was, in the deepest sense, a storyteller, a creator of fables. Sometimes the subject of the fables was a poem; sometimes it was his own immensely problematical life. The biographer seems to know nothing of his rejection of his life's work in The Rhetoric of Romanticism—*though she certainly accounts for the anxiety I noticed: a constant assertion that sometimes you publish something before you should—and you feel shame. She understands the almost comic way his past kept nipping at his heels, but she doesn't seem to understand the sense of shame. A life lived as an always threatened fiction. What stories he told. How he could* épater le bourgeois! *He knew his consciousness was shot through with fiction, with fantasy, yet he understood that that was the nature of consciousness—of all consciousness. His brilliant, illuminating stories kept him one jump ahead of in-*

sidious reality—a reality which he himself had largely created! He was a bounder, a liar, a man not to be trusted, yet in a deep sense he was a lamp. He evidently spent hours gazing at himself in mirrors. His surname means simply "The Man." What an enigma "the man" is—man is. Life—founded on nothing but lies, fictions. Yet fascinating, beautiful—not to be held down by anything. Insight is piled upon insight in his thought, he lives his life for insight, yet he believes that every insight carries with it a fundamental blindness which the thinker can never penetrate. One longs for truth, but every truth carries with it its own particular falseness. Truth and untruth are a pair that can never be separated. To be human is to tell stories. But stories are fictions. And fictions are lies.

The emotion I feel when I think about him is one of joy.

"If I had it to do over again," he said to his son, "I would have been rich."

Bounder/untrustworthy/opener of doors.

The Tiger and Other Tales

Table of Contents

Author's Note — ix

Bus Ride — 1

Sous le Pont Mirbeau — 5

The Old Man — 15

Lights — 21

The Djinn — 29

Irish — 37

The End — 39

The Adventures of Sally Phillips, Girl Detective — 43

"The Monst"	**47**
The Ern Malley Story	**59**
Families	**65**
Harry Fox (Dead) To George M. Cohan (Dead)	**69**
Broughton Fountain	**73**
My Death	**79**
An E-mail to George	**81**
Malèna	**89**
Man Wolf	**93**
The Tiger	**101**
Epilogue: Two Plays	**121**

Bus Ride

His father was of a cheerful disposition, his mother of a quite melancholy temper; both contributed to the character of the child. Do you have the time, she said. He was standing almost rooted to the spot waiting for a bus. Some are quick to notice, others require convalescence. She was not speaking to him. The bus had not arrived. I have hoped for some time, he thought, to have entered into an agreement with certain people, but the substance has rarely shown itself in ingenuity and depth. Her unmistakable body entered the bus. The light was changing slowly all around him. He stood. I have hoped for some time, he thought, to have achieved a modus operandi. Now he felt the slight chill which was the mark of the beginning of the evening. But I have failed in this. It was as if he were attempting to turn to stone. Do you know what time the next bus is, she said. He stood. She did not repeat her question. The bus, his bus, had not yet arrived. He could feel her eyes on him. He stood there, rooted, like a tree. There was a tree behind him. He had no idea what sort of tree. Sometimes, at the beginning of a story, you can sense what it was that made the writer begin that story. The beginning is always interesting. The light had changed, perceptibly. He wondered if she would repeat her question. Diphtheria. Someone was standing behind him. Each night he had stayed home hoping to have achieved some understanding. He watched carefully now, carefully. He entered the bus. No one was getting out.

After a long convalescence of three years or more he had returned to the grammar school. His word box had increased perceptibly.

SHAKESPEARE

CAMBRIDGE SELECTION

BELVEDERE

Inside there was a picture of a man and a book. Sometimes in a story one can follow the twists and turnings of an author's mind. The bus was moving in an unfamiliar landscape. He would have to go downtown. But the landscape, here, was unfamiliar. He watched as it passed by, slowly. The bus turned. It stopped. What do you think of a person in a particular way that is time, he thought. She was smiling at him but not directly. What do you think of a person who is almost forty years old and still unable to tie his shoelaces. That's what he is. Almost forty years old and still unable to tie his shoelaces. His mother has to do it for him.

She was sitting directly across from him but she had not spoken. The two women who had been speaking stopped. He wondered if there had been something he should have said. She arose and rang the bell. *As the landscape changed it became more like something he remembered.*

BUS RIDE

As a result of a great mischance he had grown up with a melancholy and irritable temperament such as belongs to men of ingenuity and depth; thanks to the one, they are quick as lightning in perception, thanks to the other, they take no pleasure in verbal cleverness or falsehood. As the landscape changed it became like something he remembered. His mother stood over him wondering what to say. He said, I don't want you to do that again. It was time. The bus stopped. Longing for the release the story promises, the writer begins. I have never done that to you, she said. Not ever. *I have never yet broken your skin when I hit you with my fists.*

The Tiger and Other Tales

Sous le Pont Mirbeau

Various writers were sent a story about a community which has a strange custom: its young men gather on Mirbeau Bridge and leap—often beautifully—into the water below. No one ever survives the leap. The story has various elements. We were asked to take at least two of them and make a story of our own. This is mine. I considered calling the story "Poor Thing."

Yes, no one survived the leap. Except one. They don't speak about it, except a few of the old ones. They're the ones that know him. Not the current crop. What do they know? Watching the telly, going to stupid films. What do they know about anything?

The old ways, ah, the old ways. You couldn't talk about it. It wasn't talk that made it. It was something else. A feeling, perhaps, but that's not it either. That's too vague. No, no, it wasn't a feeling. It was a, well, it was a presence, an aura perhaps. It's not there now. The telly and the films drive out the aura—poof. But it was there then. Not that it was any mysterious thing. It was as common as water then. We all felt it. We were all so to speak nourished by it, held in its arms—but it wasn't so what do they say "anthropocentric" as that, no it wasn't "anthropocentric" at all. It's like the water you know. You're either in it or you're not. And you know whether you're in it or not. Now people are not. But then they were in it. It held us.

The Tiger and Other Tales

Richard Thatcher was not a bad lot. Just like all of us who grew up hereabouts. One of many, no different than the others, no. I knew him when he was a lad, but he was a little older than I was, and wild. I was fond of books, always was since I learned to read, but he, he was never one to spend any time at the library. "A lot of dead words," he said. "We ought to toss them over the bridge with the leapers. They're a bad job."

What he liked was action of any kind. Sports. That was his love. Oh, he'd compete with anyone over anything. How he loved to wrestle and to run! "Where are you running, Richard?" we'd ask him. "Oh, nowhere," he said, "I'm running to run. I'm running to catch the wind and then run faster run faster." And swimming. Oh, how he could swim. "Part fish he must be," we said. "Swim, Richard! Outrace us all!" And he would. He'd ask his body to do impossible things and his body would shrug and smile and say, "Yes, Richard, I'll do it."

"God, it must be hell to be old," he said, "sitting around with your aches and pains and remembering the 'good old days' when you wasn't. The good old days! What was so good about them? You got to be old because of your fear of the leap. The brave ones, the ones with no fear—they cared for nothing. It was glory that drove them. It was glory that brought them to the bridge's edge and glory that pushed them over. Look at the beauty of their bodies, look at the marvelous shine to that young flesh as it flies out, careless, into the waiting arms of the Infinite. What is your old age to that?"

Richard Thatcher was one to go off by himself for periods. He'd scale the cliff or disappear for weeks into the wood. Just when people began to think he'd done for, just when they'd think, "He'll not come back this time," just then was when he'd show up, smiling with his big teeth and carrying a bag of berries or some fish or something to give to his mother, who had long ago given up trying to control him or even understand him. His father was one of those who had gone to glory, who had made the leap, but his mother raised him as well as she could, never complaining. Folks wondered how she was able to do it, him being so wild and all.

"Richard," she'd say to him, "why are you doing this to me, why do you make me suffer so?" "Ah, Ma," he'd say, "I'm not doing nothing. There's nothing to fear. I know, I know you worry when I go off as I do, but think of the joy when I return. Isn't there something there? Would you like it if I were nothing but a shadow following you around all the time, sticking to your apron strings? I have strength in me, life it is, and I must honor it. I must go wherever it tells me."

"And will you perish like your father in the leap? Is that where this life you call it is telling you to go? To your death? Is that your secret?" "I have no secrets, Ma. This—something—takes me over, that's all. 'The wind bloweth where it listeth,' it says in the Holy Book. That's how it is with me. I'm not doing anything apurpose. I have no desire to leap. Yet if it tells me to leap, leap I shall. And be happy doing it. Better glory, Ma, and a short life, than a slow trudging to the grave getting weaker and weaker as you go. Oh, look at those old men and then look at me. What have I got in common with them? What do they lead but lives of misery, whereas my life, Ma, my life is joy." "And a misery for those unfortunates who love you," says his mother, weeping, "a misery for me." "Oh, don't cry, Ma," says he. "Don't cry. Look at these flowers I picked for you. Do they last, Ma? Let them die if they wish. What pleasure their deaths give to others. What beauty. Take them now and joy in them." And the old woman took the flowers. But she continued to weep.

It's said that it was during one of these "trips" that Richard met something. Exactly what I could not tell you. I've never met it myself, and have no wish to. But meet it he did. It was in the woods, under a special tree, an alder, where Richard liked to stretch himself out at noontide. Just stretch himself out and sleep the sleep of an animal, more like an animal than like a man, so pure and dreamless was it. Suddenly there was a voice at his side. And it wasn't a voice exactly, especially since there was no body for the voice to come out of. But he heard it distinctly, and he had no doubt that it was real. It was as real as you or me. Realer perhaps. And it was telling him to awaken.

SOUS LE PONT MIRBEAU

Richard opened his eyes. But he saw nothing. "You need to open your inner eye to see me," said the voice. And suddenly Richard did. He saw a small animal, like a kitten, a small thing, nothing that would threaten him or anything, just a small thing. And it was speaking to him though it didn't move its lips.

"Did you enjoy your nap, Richard?" the thing asked. "Yes, indeed," said Richard. "And who are you to waken me out of it and take the joy of it away from me?" "I am no one you know and the form you see is not my form. Were you to see me as I am you would burst apart. Here I am a kitten. But in my home I'm something altogether different." "Are you human?" asked Richard. "No, I am not human," said the thing. "But I don't hate humans. I try to help them if I can." "And how have you helped them?" asked Richard. "I helped your father," said the thing. "You knew my father?" asked Richard. "I helped him," said the thing. "And what did you do to help him?" asked Richard. "I helped him to a happy death," says the thing. "I helped him in the leap to soar beautifully and to demonstrate the beauty of his young muscles and the sharpness of his young mind as he jumped magnificently onto the rocks below." "And is that what you have in mind for me then?" asked Richard. "No, I have something different in mind for you." "And what is that?" "I am going to help you be the first to survive the leap."

"No one survives the leap," says Richard, "and I can't

say I mind dying in that way, leaping to glory." "No one has *yet* survived the leap," says the thing, "but there is a way and I know it. I know how a young man can leap and live." "Then why didn't you tell it to my father?" asks Richard. "I didn't know it THEN," says the thing. "So you're capable of learning." "That's all I'm capable of doing. I have no capacity for action. What you see of me is nothing but an image projected into your mind. I am nothing but a will of the wisp, a bit of smoke, a light breeze, a nothing. Yet I know how to survive the leap." "And will you impart this information to me?" asked Richard, who was growing impatient with this repartee. "Yes," says the thing, "on one condition." "And what is that?" says Richard. "That you give me your body," says the thing. "That I live through you. I don't mean that you will vanish. Far from it. And yet—you will have me in you, too. I can do nothing unless you agree." "All right," says Richard, "I agree."

Oh, but he was a foxy man, and even as he said it he crossed his fingers and thought: "I will agree only until the sunset of the day the leap is made. After that, my spiritual friend, you're on your own. But I'll use you, yes I'll use you, to be the first to survive the leap."

"There is a place, I can show it to you," says the thing, "where the water is deep enough for a diver to survive. No one has ever found it. But I found it one day. I have great powers of sight and can see much. And one day, after your father's death, I saw that, that special place where it is possible for a leaper to leap and then live." "Show it to me!" commanded Richard. "Yes," said the thing, "look." And Richard looked, and, yes, he saw the spot, he saw it clearly though it was more than a mile off to the bridge.

It was soon after that that Richard announced his intention to make the leap during the next ceremony. His mother and a certain young woman who had eyes for him attempted to persuade him that it was folly, but he would not change his mind, though he told them nothing of the thing he had met in the forest. No, he would not change.

And what a day it was, that day he leaped. Six young men dived, but only one walked up the long path to the top afterwards. You could see the looks of amazement on the faces of the people on the bridge when he emerged from the water and then slowly made his way to rejoin them. What feasting there was then! What joy for all! And then in the midst of everything, Richard heard a voice: "You must let me ride you!" "Ride!" thought Richard, "it will only be for a short time."

And he suddenly rose up from the table and ran madly around the place, touching everything he could find, people, things, falling upon the grass, upon trees. "You're mad," thought Richard, "stop it, you fool." "You must let me ride you, ride you," said the thing. And the thing thrust Richard towards the edge of the bridge and did a dance, one foot extended over the edge, fearless. And then turned a somersault and then— But I can't tell you what happened then. It was to Richard's shame, and the very people who had cheered him suddenly began to feel revulsion for him. They began to say, "No one has ever survived the leap. No one can survive it. I don't believe he did it. It must have been fakery. We have been deceived. He is a madman and a deceiver at once." And Richard, struggling, said, "Get out of me, you foul spirit, get ye gone, I crossed my fingers when I agreed, it was not valid, I agreed to only a day's occupancy of my body, and, look, the sun is just now beginning to set."

"I bargained in good faith," said the spirit, "you are a deceiver." "There are powers stronger than you, spirit, and I will invoke them if you try to occupy me a moment beyond sunset." The spirit knew what Richard said was true. There were powers stronger than he.

"You think you have won over me," said the spirit, "but you have not." Suddenly, the entire crowd of people had the same idea or heard the same voice speaking: "Richard Thatcher is a deceiver, he has not truly jumped, let him prove himself now, let him jump while we all watch. If not, we will throw him from the bridge ourselves." Richard understood what was happening. "I don't need you, spirit," he said, "I know the spot. I will jump the moment after sunset." "Good riddance!" cried the spirit, "just like your father!" Richard ran to the bridge and jumped just as the sun went down on the horizon. His body crashed on the rocks below. Suddenly everyone there heard a ghastly laughter which left each of them horrorstricken. They went to their graves remembering that sound.

And so Richard Thatcher is never spoken of. But, if you believe such things, and no doubt you do not, there is a spirit in the wood which can tell you where to leap so that you too, like Richard Thatcher, can survive. But the spirit is a wild spirit. It has never learned to live in human company. Richard's body, filled as it was with his *élan vital*, was too intense. In any case, the spirit's laughter turned to moans, and I expect that it would be less likely, these days, to strike a bargain.

The Tiger and Other Tales

The Old Man

Everyone knew the old man. Some feared him. Most knew him only vaguely. He seemed never to have been young. He stayed there in his old house, rarely venturing out except for necessities. Never speaking to anyone. If he had a relative, no one knew it. If he had a pet, no one saw it. And yet they knew him—or felt they did—as he went about his business. He was cordial, oh yes, cordial to everyone. But rarely warm. Did women interest the old man? Did men? Did children? Did anything interest him except his own closed existence, as he pattered around? "Thank you, Mr. Garrett," he said, paying the grocer. "Thank you, I'm fine. I don't need help." And off he went. My mother said he was old to her—that she couldn't remember him ever being any younger. If he had a youth, she said, it must have been somewhere else. Unimaginable.

Yet he was part of the fabric of the town. No one minded him. No one thought much of his grizzled appearance. *Does he bathe?* said Emily Thompson, *I don't think he bathes. Does he pray?* asked Philip Leroy. *I've never seen him at church. What does he eat?* asked Sally Miller. *Oh, some biscuits, vegetables, occasionally meat; told me once he liked to cook*, said Mr. Garrett. *Maybe he's a faggot*, said Mr. Brownstone. *Faggots cook. So do ordinary men*, said Mr. Garrett, *I like to cook myself. Are you a faggot?* asked Mr. Brownstone. *No*, said Mr. Garrett.

    This old man knew a woman who hated cats. She was fearful that one might move close to her, pretending love, and suddenly strike at her. If she saw a cat on the sidewalk she would immediately cross the street. The woman was not old but middle-aged. She had never married. She had a secretarial job in the near-by city and returned each day by train. She rarely saw the old man but she would occasionally phone him. Their conversations were brief and superficial. The old man talked about his aches and pains, considerable at this time of life. The woman spoke of her day at the office and of the ways in which her co-workers, who were for the most part decent enough people, thought her strange. To tell the truth, she thought herself strange. Her emotional life was a complete mystery. She didn't know why or how her emotions arose. Yet she felt them deeply. She liked the old man because he was as clueless about his emotions as she was about hers. When they spoke on the phone they could pretend to an intimacy which each realized they did not share.

    One day the middle-aged woman killed the old man. It was not a premeditated murder. She decided to go to his house and pay him a call. She didn't phone first; the old man was always home. He didn't receive her with pleasure, but, remembering their phone calls, put up as good a front as he could, offering her tea and a biscuit. The

THE OLD MAN

woman suddenly felt a strange revulsion. The old man looked at her with his ancient, red-tinged eyes. He began to whine about his life, as he did on the phone. The woman realized at that moment what their bond was: it was hatred, hatred of themselves, hatred of others. The old man moved slowly, like a cat, and she hated cats. She picked up a heavy skillet while his back was turned and smashed it as hard as she could on the old man's head. He went down with a grunt. The movement was so sudden and unexpected and the pain so intense that he didn't feel surprise. He just died, blood spurting out of his skull.

The woman had hoped that she would feel pleasure from her act, or at least release, but she did not. She felt horror and then an unexpected tenderness towards the old man. She reached out her hand to his dead form and began to caress his shoulder. The old man, who was dead, felt nothing. His soul soared upward but no further than the ceiling. From its perch on the ceiling, the old man's soul looked down at the woman's tenderness. It felt a sudden flush of pity for her. His soul was naked and needed a body in which it could lodge. It swooped down into the woman. She felt its presence with great joy. She suddenly understood why certain tribes devour their enemies or why certain people eat red meat. Suddenly she *was* the old man. His soul inhabited her. Yet she did not cease to be herself.

The Tiger and Other Tales

The woman rose from her handiwork and thought whether anyone had seen her come to the old man's house. She felt certain that no one had. She would make certain that no one saw her leave. The woman now had two souls and two intellects inhabiting her. She was stronger than she had ever been. And she was androgynous. She reached down into the old man's pants and found his penis. With a large kitchen knife she tenderly removed it. She washed it lovingly in the old man's sink and dried it with a paper towel. She put it in a plastic bag and stuffed it into her purse. It was hers now. She gave a prayer of thanks to the old man for the offering he had inadvertently made to her. Upon the reception of the penis, the old man's soul gave a cry of happiness which the woman felt throughout her body. There was a shudder, and she realized she was having an orgasm.

The woman returned to her home, safe in the knowledge of her act. When the police came to question her, she said she occasionally telephoned the old man but rarely saw him—and that she had not seen him at all recently. She could not imagine why someone would want to kill him. The police thanked her and went away. Then the old man's soul began to whisper things to her. At first they were simple compliments: *You're looking very beautiful today. I like your hair that way.* Then they became suggestions. *Why don't you wear a rose with that outfit. You know,*

THE OLD MAN

if you wore that green blouse with that blue skirt, I would love you even more. The woman was flattered by these compliments and wished to please the old man. *And your underwear,* said the old man's soul, *I wish you would get some nicer underwear. Something red, for example.* The woman began to ask the old man's soul what she should wear during the day: *Blue panties today, the ones with the flowers on them. Black today. Oh, you need a new bra. Let me touch your breasts.* And the woman shuddered under his touch. People noticed the change in the middle-aged woman, but they could not account for it. *It must be the menopause,* they thought. *Blue today, black tomorrow.*

The middle-aged woman began to believe that she had not murdered the old man; she had simply transformed him. His history had become her history, his thoughts her thoughts. His penis, which she froze, remained in the refrigerator amid the ice cream and the frozen dinners. She was in ecstasy for much of the day but kept that fact from her co-workers. Though she had many orgasms, she grew wonderful at dissimulation and indirection. *How are you? Just fine, fine.* (*I am a bride of darkness. I am a nun in love with God. At the end of the world, my husband, who has never left me, will come for me with a great sword. He will cut me in half. This pain will also be a joy. And then he will weld us together so that we cannot be separated. My life will be perfect then, though it is also perfect now. My love, at long last, will have been consummated; I will be* alive.)

At 65, the woman retired and grew old, living apart from people as the old man had. Her secret was never discovered. When she died at the age of eighty-eight, she left no will, no indication of the change that had occurred in her consciousness. People noticed her death only as they might have noticed the casual separation of a leaf from a tree or a page from a notebook.

These are the facts: a middle-aged woman murders an old man by banging his head with a skillet; the murder, which was almost comical, was never solved by the police, who in any case investigated it only in the most lackadaisical way. No one cared very much about the old man. When the woman's soul died, the man's soul died with her. Both vanished into a nothingness which I must believe had been prepared for them at the beginning of the world. But perhaps this statement is untrue. Perhaps both souls exist in a state so different from the human that we could see it directly in front of us and still not recognize it. Perhaps their love remains in that state. But here, their story vanishes, just as everything vanishes. First the old man. Then the woman and the murder. Then the love. Then I.

Lights

"I suppose it would be all right," said his father.

Night had fallen. The quality of his vision shifted.

"...*if* there were some way we could manage it."

"There is, I'm sure there is."

"Well how do we know he'll be there?"

"He'll be there I'm sure of it."

"And if he is there how do you know that he'll agree—"

"I'll find some way to convince him, all you have to do is introduce me."

They were sitting near to one another in the living room. The son's voice was slightly louder than his father's.

"And what of Mother—do we tell her?"

"No, there'll be no need for that. She'll find out soon enough."

"*If* it all works out."

"I know it will."

Mr. Ferguson was sitting by his car. He was waiting his turn to enter the car wash.

"Hello, Mr. Ferguson."

The Tiger and Other Tales

"Hello?"

Mr. Ferguson was not certain he knew the man who was speaking his name. He arose and adjusted his glasses.

"How interesting to find you here, Mr. Ferguson."

"Yes?"

"Have you ever met my son, Everett?"

Everett smiled at him. "Hello, Mr. Ferguson."

Mr. Ferguson a tall thin man in a white suit adjusted his glasses again.

"Hello, ah, Everett."

"My son has a business proposition for you, Mr. Ferguson."

Mr. Ferguson looked hard at Everett but said nothing. Finally: "Yes…"

"He'd like to become your…typist. He's learned how at school."

"You see, sir, I'd like to learn to be a writer like you. I'm an excellent typist. I'm used to handling my father's papers. I'd like to become your *secretary*."

They were standing there in the late afternoon sun. three figures casting long deep shadows. Mr. Ferguson: "Well, I do get a lot of mail…" Was persuaded.

"But he barely knows the man," said his mother. "How can he go and live with him?"

LIGHTS

"Well it's only during the week," said Mr. Martin. "He'll be here on weekends."

"I suppose he thinks he's going to make him into a bigtime writer too."

"I don't think so. It's just a way of finding out about the business that's all. It just seemed so easy—a bigtime writer living right here in town and me knowing him a little. How can he lose? Besides, he says he'll give half of the money he makes to us."

Mrs. Martin considered for a moment.

"Well, I guess it'll be all right," she said. "He's always had ambition anyway." There was a momentary silence in which she stared with her great grey eyes at Mr. Martin. She then repeated herself. "He's always had ambition anyway."

Mr. Ferguson stared at him oddly. There was a heaviness in the air which he could not quite identify. He felt tired. Everett was repeating what he had just said. Everett put down his pencil. "That's enough of that. Do you think you could get the mail now?" said Otis Ferguson.

"I took the liberty of putting it on your desk this morning," Everett replied.

"Oh did you."

"Yes."

There was a pause. "You know I'm not sure there is enough here for you to do…"

"I'll be sure to find things, you'll see. It will free you to write more."

Mr. Ferguson stared at him oddly. There was a heaviness in the air which he could not quite identify. He felt tired.

"There are so many things to be written I feel sometimes that I can barely live to complete them all," said Everett. Mr. Ferguson turned, the heaviness upon him. "I think sometimes that there are only a *few* stories and we tell them endlessly. Each of us has his own few and we do nothing but repeat them as we write." The heaviness was becoming genuinely oppressive now. "The same words and gestures constantly returning to plague us no matter how much we believe we have avoided them. Boringly repetitive." He stared around him wondering if it would be possible to avoid this day as one avoids a boring channel on the television. He wanted to drink. Water.

"…but the mail…" said Everett, who was genuinely disturbed by this turn of the conversation.

"WHY DID I TAKE YOU ON ANYWAY," said Mr. Ferguson.

"Because I asked you to. Because you felt I could be of service to you."

"OF WHAT SORT OF SERVICE COULD YOU BE." The air

LIGHTS

became more and more oppressive. Mr. Ferguson stood up and began to pace. "What can you do for me? Can you put words in my mouth where no words are? Can you give me back the only thing that ever mattered to me—my *dis*satisfaction? What can you do for me but open my mail and talk about the weather?" Mr. Ferguson stopped moving. "I'm sorry," he said. "There is no point in saying these things to you I know." Outside a bird swooped down momentarily, avoiding the house.

"There is work to be done."

He had felt ashamed at his outburst yet felt that there was nothing he could have done about it. The oppressiveness had been intense. He had not known how to deal with it. It remained in the air like a kind of laconic echo.

"I just want to know what they're doing there that's all."

"What do you mean you want to know what they're doing there? He's giving you his money isn't he?"

"Not the money. I just want to know that's all."

A bird swooped down to feed on a flower outside their door.

"When I ask him," said Mrs. Martin, "he never says anything. He never says anything at all. I'd like to know just what he's writing in that book. I'll bet to heaven he's writing about *us*."

The Tiger and Other Tales

Lights go up and down in memory. What are the chances of finding power and redress? Her way of life was aimless, hopeless to speak of her. Otis Ferguson moved carefully in the bathroom drying each portion of his long thin body with an extraordinary lightness of touch. At last he put on his bathrobe stepped outside and began to read in the sun.

...straight through everything to the very core of *one's own being*...carries the life and fable of man nearer and nearer to order, beauty, grace, and meaning—all of which must always remain correctable in details—revised, improved, refined, enlarged, extended. Intelligence *is* arriving into the fable of the life of man.[1]

In the darkness Mrs. Martin crouched down in the bushes outside his window. She lifted herself carefully and stared inside. The scene she beheld had the unreal quality of a television program without the sound. Once again the men were silent. Otis Ferguson sat on a chair, his long legs sprawled out in front of him. Everett lay on his back on the couch in a pose Mrs. Martin had seen a thousand times over in her own home. They might have been listening to music but she could hear nothing. Finally Mr. Ferguson stood up spat crossed the room and went out. Mrs. Mar-

---

[1] William Saroyan, "A Writer's Declaration."

LIGHTS

tin put her hand to the chimney and felt the cold brick.

"That was all that was all," she said later. "Just sitting there again except for that one time when he spat into his handkerchief and went out."

Her husband looked at her with disgust. "Madge, this has got to stop. You've been sneaking around back and forth to that house for this past week. You can't do that."

"I've *been* doing it. A mother's got a right to know what her son's been doing."

"Not when she's sneaking around looking in at somebody's window she doesn't."

"How else can I find out what I need to know?"

"You might *ask* him."

"What good would that do? He'd just sit there and say nothing like he did the last time I asked him. That wouldn't do any good at all."

"Well if you ask *me* nothing is just what he's been doing—just sitting in a room and doing nothing and getting paid for it. This Ferguson is—eccentric. He's lonely and he needs...companionship."

"Eccentric is he. *No*body ever paid *no*body to sit still and do *noth*ing," said Mrs. Martin. "I'm going back!"

In the darkness Mrs. Martin looked in. The two men sat motionless across from one another in the living room.

Neither one spoke. It seemed to her that they had the unreality of figures on a TV screen when the sound is off. She watched. Nothing...

She held her body against him, hard, in the doorway. Her large eyes looked up at him. (This is a memory of Mr. and Mrs. Martin.) He moved his hand along her shoulder, down the arch of her back pressed her cunt against his cock. She closed her eyes, said, Not here. He said, Where? She (pointing): There— In the dark window, nothing—

THE DJINN

A TALE, A FABLE

Mahmud Cemaleddin Hasan Effendi was known to be perfect. *Kamal*—"perfect." He was in fact the very Pole Star of perfection. Never did an unworthy thought cross his mind; never did an unworthy word cross his lips. He had instructed others all day today and he was greatly fatigued. It was no sin to desire rest, and he thought with great delight of his warm bed as he crossed over the grass to his simple dwelling. As he neared the house, he noticed the wondrous fig tree that grew before it. It pleased him to think that he and that tree had grown old together. Its branches beckoned to him like the arms of his mother. Indeed, many were the days when his mother sat on the grass watching him as he, a child, climbed the tree. "You are closer to heaven, my son," said his mother. "But be careful not to fall to earth again." She was known far and wide to be a good woman, and when she passed from this vale of sorrows, many were the tears that were shed in that town. He could feel her warmth as he approached the tree.

What he did not notice was the djinn who just now inhabited the tree. But the djinn saw him and laughed silently.

"Good afternoon, good sir," said the djinn. "May the wondrous light that bursts forth from the eyes of the Prophet (blessed be his name!) shine upon you."

"Good afternoon, djinn," said the holy man. "I hope you are doing God's will today."

"On what day would I not be doing God's will, good sir," answered the djinn politely.

"I have…shall we say…various reports of djinns," said the holy man.

"Oh, Effendi, these tales are gross exaggerations. We have our rotten apples, of course—what group does not?—but in general we are a God-loving lot. Praise be to Allah for everything, everything. What wonders does he not perform?"

"Praise be to him, djinn."

"Still, I do have a problem, Effendi. I am in love with a young woman of good family and high reputation. And she is to be married tomorrow. What can I do, Effendi. My heart aches with such sorrow. All I wish is to tell her of my passion. I know she does not return it. But I would feel such relief if only she could hear of it. But, alas, I cannot force my tongue to utter the words."

"That is truly a sorrow, djinn," said the Perfect One.

"But you, Effendi, I have heard you speak with such eloquence that the angels came down to earth to listen and wondered whether they were in heaven again to hear such sounds. Perhaps, Effendi, *you* could tell her. It would

THE DJINN

be a great relief to me—just so that she knows that I, a peace-loving djinn, love her as deeply as a djinn can love anything. Oh, please, Effendi."

"Well, I might write her a note..."

"No, no, Efffendi, you must *tell* her. It must be her ear's hearing. And it must be tonight since she marries tomorrow."

"Well, I suppose..."

"It would do me *so* much good, O Perfect One. My soul would at last be at peace. Please follow me. Her home is not far."

With that the djinn climbed down from the tree and motioned the holy man to follow him.

Slowly they made their way through the dark town. Finally they came to the woman's house. It was a warm night, and her window was open.

"Say this," said the djinn: " 'O beauteous one! Answer I beg of you!' "

"O beauteous one! Answer I beg of you!" said the holy man.

A window was opened. A shrewish voice said, "Who calls out to me?"

"Say, 'I, O beauteous one! I, the djinn who loves you with all his heart.' "

"I, O beauteous one! I, the djinn who loves you with all his heart," said the holy man.

"The Holy Koran says you are made of smokeless flame," said the woman. And with that she threw a pot at the holy man. Her aim was good, and she hit her target. But she could not see the djinn, only the holy man.

"But Sweetest of all Sweet Things, O..."

And with that she threw a raw egg, which also hit the target.

"You must climb in her window," said the djinn. "She is angry now, but when she sees you standing in front of her she will recognize your holiness and listen."

"Climb in the window!" said the holy man.

"Yes, yes," said the djinn, and pushed him forward.

The holy man was not used to climbing into windows and it cost him some effort to do so, especially since the woman beat at his knuckles as he scrambled at the sill. Finally, he was inside.

"Woman," he said, "this djinn—" But he got no further. The woman's mother was suddenly upon him. She was a large woman, and she pinned him to the floor.

"I am not speaking for myself," cried out the holy man in desperation. "I am speaking for that djinn."

"What djinn?" said the woman as she looked out the window. No one was there. "There is no djinn here."

"No djinn?" said the holy man.

"Only a most foolish old man," said the woman. "Don't you know the deceptions djinns can weave?"

"Well, I have heard—"

THE DJINN

"You have heard right. You are a foolish old man. Somewhere out there in the night, the djinn is laughing at us all. I myself am in the deepest of trouble. I am a foolish young woman and I allowed my deep love to get the better of me. My lover is gone, and I am with child, and there is no one to marry me."

"No one to marry you?" said the holy man, gasping a little from his position on the floor.

"No one," answered the woman.

At these sad words the woman's mother began to weep. She released her hold on the holy man.

"You—you're not getting married tomorrow?"

"No, of course not," said the woman harshly. "Whoever put that lie into your mouth?"

The holy man was silent for a moment. Finally he said softly, "I am without a wife."

"What?" said the woman in surprise. "You would marry me?"

"I would," said the holy man, "for as I spoke the djinn's words, I realized the truth of them—I saw you through his eyes, in all your radiance. You are as beautiful and pure as the taste of water. Oh, what a thing it would be for me, at my age, to have a child. Though I follow the will of Allah in all things, I have been so lonely. A wife and a child would be the hope and perfection of my old age."

With that the woman smiled and kissed the holy man. Together they heard the echo of a not unkindly laughter that rang through the night. "All of us," said the holy man, "djinns and men, perform the will of Allah. How alive with meaning the night is. And tomorrow you, love, will be my bride."

The woman smiled. The djinn, who was far away now, far out into the night, had kept his solemn promise to his love. *Kamal.*

Epilogue

My world was coastal
The vast Atlantic near at hand
My ancestors
Wandered
And were "uncontrollable"
I come promising
Night languages
Blinding suns
Lies
The moon—
I thought your world
Dust
And yearning:
Land of horsemen, swords, and palm trees
Land of learning
And the incalculable
Ambiguities
Of the real.

THE DJINN

Do you dream you can rule deep water?
Our promises
Rise
Transforming us.
I am passing
Like a wave
Like a particle of dust
Like a leaf.
Let the deceptions of love
Blossom
In these precise moments
Of daring and uncertainty.
I breathe in dust.
We will be gone—yes?
"Highest good
Is like water."

The Tiger and Other Tales

IRISH

What does it mean to be Irish? Or, more specifically, what does it mean to be Irish-American?

To get from my house to Cornell University where I was a freshman in 1958, you drove up the hypotenuse of a right triangle. My father, who had been born in New York State farm country in 1895 and who grew up with the automobile, drove up the two sides of the triangle, thinking they were the hypotenuse. He never quite trusted that machine to get him where he wanted to go, and before any trip of consequence he would fortify himself with "a few drops of the craythur."

As we neared Cornell, there were several small towns which regularly made money at this time of year by giving tickets to students blazing through them on their way back to school. My father never blazed anywhere, but he did accidentally turn left through a red light as we slowly made our way to our goal. Suddenly a motorcycle policeman was upon us. The policeman said—and I don't exaggerate his brogue—"HO WHERE YA GOIN'?" My father pulled over to the side of the road and said very politely, "Gee, officer, did I go through that red light? I'm sorry. I won't do it again. Say," he said, "are you Irish?" The policeman flushed and said, rather testily, "Well, I'm Irish, what of it?" "Well," said my father, "we're Irish too. Meet the boy. We're taking him up to his freshman year at Cornell University."

My mother, who was Italian, said not a word.

By the time the conversation between my father and the policeman was over there was no longer any question of a ticket. The policeman was inviting us to his home for coffee and to "meet the wife." My father politely declined and said he would "drop by on his way back."

I have no idea whether my father even knew the name of the town whose laws he was violating, and I certainly do not. But when he heard that accent, he knew exactly how to behave. He acknowledged the policeman's authority: "Gee, officer, did I go through that red light? I'm sorry. I won't do it again." But he then invoked a *higher* authority: "Are you Irish?"

There was a joke my father liked to tell, and perhaps its moral figured in that Irish cop's reaction to us. The Irish maid is about to leave for the day when the master says to her, "Mary, this is terrible. Look at the dust on this table. I can write my name in the dust." "Oh, sir," she says, misunderstanding, "ain't education grand!" Perhaps the thought of "education," and particularly education for the Irish, was "grand" for that Irish cop too. "Meet the boy," said my father proudly, "we're taking him up to his freshman year at Cornell University."

What does it mean to be Irish? What does it mean to be Irish-American?

THE END

The two close friends had been arguing all afternoon. They were also laughing at the absurdity of their argument. The argument was all in the script. They were radio stars, Fred Allen and Jack Benny. The argument—they called it a "feud"—was all in the writing. It was the late 1940s. Everyone knew that it would soon be The End of radio. Allen knew it. Benny knew it. The script writers knew it. All the comedians figured that they had better start wearing dresses like Milton Berle. They had better start squirting each other with seltzer bottles. It didn't matter what they said anymore. Nothing like that mattered. You had to *look* funny.

When it was radio, no one paid any attention to what anyone looked like. William Conrad, a short, fat, balding man who played Matt Dillon on *Gunsmoke*, thought he would go on to play Matt Dillon on television. After all, he had made movies. He knew how to act in front of a camera. But only his voice was six foot tall and ruggedly handsome. He was a short, fat radio actor. James Arness got the part. That's how it was in those days. The money moved what moved and the money was being taken out of radio and being put into television.

"You, uh, you *finished* tonight, didn't you, Jack," said Allen to Benny in the script. Benny had, for the season.

"Yes," said Jack carelessly. "Every year the sponsor and I say goodbye and shake hands and...*yikes!*" "What's wrong?" asked Allen. "This year he didn't shake hands." Whoo hoo it was funny. Darkness was descending on radio, which had encouraged everybody to "turn out your lights." The brightly lit radio dials were on the wane. "I don't care about TV," people would say, "I'll stick with radio." "TV is good for shut-ins, not for regular people." (Why was radio not good for shut-ins?) The great radio producer William Spier gave people buttons that said, *Help stamp out TV*, recalling a slogan of the time, *Help stamp out TB*.

For a while, Fred Allen was king of the airwaves. Then it was discovered how to destroy him. Not just win; destroy him. His competition *gave away money*. That's what the audience really cares about. That's what the bourgeoisie has in its bones. If you listened and you knew the name of a song, they would give you money. But you had to listen. That's how Fred Allen went down. Intellectual wit came bang against moneygreed and lost, lost, lost.

The poet wrote: *The idea is that there is a link between self-criticism, feelings of worthlessness, and bourgeois morality. Is that possible? Does the one feed upon the other? Feelings of terrible self-criticism, worthlessness are in their way socially unacceptable. Bourgeois morality is extremely socially acceptable. Is it possible that the one* masks *itself as the other—and thus achieves a permanence and a place of honor in one's consciousness? Is it possible that bourgeois morality and feelings of worthlessness,*

THE END

even of self-destruction, are, at base, one and the same? Bourgeois morality brought old radio down.

"To stay on the air, you gotta give stuff away," said Allen from the script, remembering his audience. "I've got a new quiz show; it's called 'Break the Contestant.'" So, ha ha, in the script, Benny "disguises himself"—this wasn't hard to do on radio!—and enters Allen's contest. He wins! But no, he has been recognized. "You're king for a day!" says Allen, mocking Benny in the script. "Come on, men, the king has to have new robes. *Take off his pants.*" This was radio, but it had an audience of people watching. This show gave those people something to see. It was like Milton Berle wearing a dress. "Allen," snarled Benny as his pants were removed, "you haven't seen The End of me!" "No, king, I haven't," said Allen, "but *it's coming up soon.* Good night, folks, we're a little late."

The Tiger and Other Tales

The Adventures of Sally Phillips, Girl Detective

Episode #5379½

ANNOUNCER: The lithe, golden-haired teenager sits at a desk. Before her are pages of complicated mathematical symbols. Suddenly the phone rings.

[ringing]

SALLY: Sally Phillips, Girl Detective. Oh, hello, Uncle Mortimer.

UNCLE MORTIMER: No time to talk, Sally. Murder has been committed. We need your help.

SALLY: Oh, gee, Uncle Mortimer. I've got a trigonometry test tomorrow morning.

UNCLE MORTIMER: No time for trig, Sally. We need you *now*. Uh!

[silence]

ANNOUNCER: The phone is dead. And so perhaps is Uncle Mortimer. It's time for another thrilling adventure of *Sally Phillips, Girl Detective*!

Organ Music.

ANNOUNCER: Yes, boys and girls, Sally will be here in a moment. But first, we want to tell you about the new, vitamin-fortified, dee-licious cereal, Montague's Mottled Oats. Yes, boys and girls, mom will be happy to see all the strength you gain from those healthy vitamins in every bite of Montague's Mottled Oats. And you'll love the flavor too! Gosh, those tasty bits are every bit as good as diving into a little stream on a summer's day. Yessir. What do you think of Montague's Mottled Oats, Sally?

SALLY: Oh, Mr. Averbach, I eat them every morning. That great flavor and those healthy vitamins give me the strength to go out and have adventures. My mom tells me that Montague's Mottled Oats are just what I need to grow up to be a healthy mother and wife.

ANNOUNCER: Thank you, Sally. Boys and girls, you too will be satisfied with Montague's Mottled Oats. Remember: We try em out on horses.

[sound of whinnying]

And now: The Adventures of Sally Phillips, Girl Detective.

You remember, boys and girls, when we last saw our friends, Sally and her companion Ramrod, they were being driven home by their faithful Italian driver, Antonio.

[Sound of car: whirr whirr]

RAMROD: Gosh, Sal, that was some adventure with those foreign spies.

THE ADVENTURES OF SALLY PHILLIPS, GIRL DETECTIVE

SALLY: Yes, Ram, it certainly was. Say, Ram, did you notice that black sedan that seems to be following us?

RAMROD: No, Sal, I didn't.

ANTONIO: Yes, but-a I did, Miss-a Sal. Atsa no good, I think. I'm-a saw the flash o light from that-a car. I'm-a think that's a gun a flash.

RAMROD: What did he say? Something about a gun.

SALLY: Yes, Antonio, I think you're right. And wasn't that whiz we heard a minute ago a shot?

ANTONIO: I'm-a think it-a was a shot too. Look-a the hole inna da wind-a shield.

RAMROD: What did he say, Sally?

SALLY: We're being shot at, Ram. [gunshot] It would be a good idea to return the fire. That black sedan's been following us for the past six miles.

RAMROD: Oh, *them*. Ok, Sal, just let me get my trusty pistol.

[gunshot]

SALLY: Good shot, Ram. You hit the front tire. Oh, oh. They're out of control.

ANTONIO: You bet-a they out of control if-a they shoot-a at us.

SALLY: Oh! They're swerving into that tree. Oh, Ram, I can't look.

[sound of crash]

RAMROD: They've crashed, Sally.

SALLY: Oh!

ANNOUNCER: Yes, boys and girls, Sally and Ram are off on another adventure. Who are the people in that black sedan, and why were they shooting at our friends? Will any of them survive the car wreck, and, if they do, will they offer any clues? Tune in tomorrow at this same time to hear the answers to these and other important questions. You'll hear Antonio say, "They crazy-a people those-a guys!" And Ramrod say, "What did he say?" And Sally say, "Oh! Ramrod! This is a fine kettle of fish." That's all in tomorrow's *Adventures of Sally Phillips, beautiful, lithe, golden-haired, teenage girl detective*—brought to you by Montague's Mottled Oats, the cereal that horses (and mothers) like best.

[sound of whinnying]

Organ music.

"The Monst"

The ground slips when the monster comes along.
—Rosamond Purcell, *Special Cases*

The D D D Monster was worried.

He wanted very much to be a part of the family he was living with but he wasn't sure exactly where he fit in. Most families have mothers, fathers, children, relatives, dogs, cats, goldfish—but monsters? How did monsters fit into a family? He tried to calm himself by extending his forefinger and poking it gently into the sofa three times while saying "D D D," which is how he got his name. Nobody, including the monster, knew *why* he said "D D D" and poked things. He just said it and poked. Usually he liked to do this very much. It made him feel *very* good. So he tried again: "D D D." But it didn't help. He was still worried.

The Astronaut often assured the Monster that he was cared for, and the Monster always believed the Astronaut. But the Monster wanted more than assurance. He wanted to be a real member of the family, just as the Astronaut was. The Astronaut's father, Jack, would call the Astronaut "big boy" and "my son." Who was there to call the D D D Monster such names? Maybe monsters didn't have families.

"Shut up, D," said the Astronaut, walking into the room. That was the Astronaut's way of greeting the Monster. The Monster liked it because it meant the Astronaut had noticed him. Usually the greeting made the Monster say something. But today he was more than usually sad. "Thank you, Sean," he said—he always thanked the Astronaut when the Astronaut told him to shut up—but he said nothing more.

"What's the matter, Monst?" asked Sean, who noticed the Monster's sadness.

"Wah," said the Monster. "I'm not a member of the familyyyyyyy. Wah."

Sean poked the Monster to cheer him up. "D D D," he said. Usually this made the monster feel *very* good. But today it didn't seem to work.

"I tell you what, Monst," said Sean. "Let's go ask Jack whether you're a member of the family. He'll be sure to know."

So the Astronaut and the Monster went in search of Jack, the Astronaut's father. The problem here was that Jack really didn't know whether the Monster were a member of the family. The Monster *looked* quite a lot like Jack—in fact, he looked almost *exactly* like Jack. But that didn't necessarily qualify him as a member of the family. The world, after all, has many people who look a great deal like us, but they aren't necessarily *related* to us. Jack had no idea where the Monster had come from. One day he

"THE MONST"

was simply *there*, that's all, walking around in his funny, rolling way and poking people while saying "D D D." Jack's wife Adelle wondered whether that were some sort of code, but it didn't seem to be. So when the Monster and the Astronaut approached Jack to ask him their question, he didn't really know how to answer.

"Well," said Jack, "you do look quite a bit like me."

"Yeah, yeah," said the Monster excitedly.

"And people who look like you are often related to you."

"Yeah, yeah, yeah," said the Monster.

"But then, people who look a *lot* like you are sometimes not related to you at all."

"Oh," said the Monster, becoming considerably less enthusiastic.

"So, while there's a good *chance* you're related to me—"

"Look," said the Astronaut, suddenly having an idea. "We have a dog. Isn't the dog a member of the family?"

"Why, yes," said Jack, "certainly the dog is a member of the family."

"And we have a goldfish," said the Astronaut. "Isn't the goldfish a member of the family?"

"Of course he is," said Jack.

"Yeah, yeah," said the D D D Monster, brightening a little.

"Well, we also have a *monster*," said the Astronaut. "Isn't the monster a member of the family?"

"Why, yes," said Jack. "I hadn't looked at it that way. Yes, he is."

"Monst," said Sean, "you're the family monster."

"Yeah, yeah," said the Monster.

"Kind of like the family dog," said Sean, "only better cause we don't have to walk you."

"Yeah, yeah, yeah," said the Monster.

"Well, that's settled," said the Astronaut. "Monst, would you like me to D D D you?"

"Yeah, *yeah*," said the Monster.

And so Sean put out his finger and poked the Monster in his tummy, saying, "D D D."

"Thank you, thank you, Sean," said the Monster. "Thank you for proving I'm a member of the family."

Sean smiled and said, "Shut up, D."

And for once the Monster shut up.

Editor's note: It is not certain whether the D D D Monster has to be walked or not.

Today the Monster decided to write a poem. He was rather a formal Monster, and he decided to make it a formal poem. He decided he would write a haiku. The Astronaut had learned about haiku at school, and he had carefully instructed the DDD Monster in how to do it. "The first line is five syllables," said the Astronaut. "The second line is seven syllables. And the third line is five syllables again. It's easy."

But it wasn't so easy for the Monster. The problem was that he could go to three pretty easily. His DDD's were like that. But getting to five and then seven was much harder. He tried and he tried. Finally the Astronaut helped him. This was the haiku he produced:

> DDDDD
> DDDDDDD
> DDDDD.

Everyone congratulated him, so, with another mighty effort, he produced still another haiku. This one went

> DDDDD
> DDDDdDD
> DDDDD.

That, however, was the end of the DDD Monster's career as a poet.

The DDD Monster was disturbed again. He was looking for his opinion. He knew he had one, but he wasn't quite sure what or where it was. He thought it might show up if he just looked hard enough. He knew it would be a good opinion.

"What's the matter, Monst?" asked the Astronaut.

"I am looking for my opinion," said the Monster.

"Looking for your opinion, eh," said the Astronaut. "Any idea where you might have left it?"

"No," said the Monst. "Jack was talking to someone and he turned to me and he asked, 'Monst, do you have an opinion?'"

"And what did you say?"

"I said of course I had an opinion. I was sure that every Monster had an opinion."

"Uh huh. And now you can't find it."

"Yeah, yeah," said the Monster. "Do you think you can help me?"

"Well, now, I just might be able to," said the Astronaut. "Come with me."

The Astronaut led the Monster into the kitchen and opened the refrigerator door. He reached in and got out some chocolate ice cream. He put some in a bowl for the Monster and some in a bowl for himself.

"Well," said the Astronaut. "Do you like that, D?"

"Oh, *yes*," said the Monster.

"Would you say it was *very good*?" asked the Astronaut, finishing up his portion.

"Oh, *yes*," said the Monster.

"Well, then," said the Astronaut. "That's your opinion."

"That's it?" said the Monster.

"That's it," said the Astronaut. "If someone asks you for

your opinion, you can say, "I think chocolate ice cream is *very good*. That's my opinion."

"Oh, thank you!" said the Monster.

"Think nothing of it," said the Astronaut.

"What was my opinion again?" asked the Monster.

"*Very good*," said the Astronaut.

"Oh, yeah."

The Monster was very happy. That was his opinion.

"Oh, now I understand," said the little girl in the schoolyard to Jack. "*You* are the D D D Monster."

"No, no, I'm not," said Jack, who had been telling her about the Monster's activities. "I just *look* a lot like him."

The question of the D D D Monster's identity was a thorny one around the Foley household. "After all," Jack reasoned, "just because someone *looks* like you doesn't make him the *same* as you."

"*You* are the D D D Monster," said the little girl, unmoved by Jack's assertion.

"We'll ask Sean about that when he gets here," said Jack.

Soon the Astronaut appeared. "Sean," said his father, "tell Mary here who the D D D Monster is."

"*You* are the D D D Monster," said Sean.

The Tiger and Other Tales

"I thought so!" said Mary triumphantly as she ran off to join her mother, who had just arrived.

"Sean," said Jack, waving to Mary's mother. "How can you say that? Do *I* go around poking people with my fingers? Do *I* go around with a bewildered look on my face? Do *I* sing *Do do do* all the time? No. How can I be the D D D Monster?"

"You *play* the D D D Monster," said Sean.

"Play the Monster!" said Jack, as if this were the most ridiculous thing he had ever heard. "We'll see when we get home."

At home, the Monst was walking around with a bewildered look on his face. He was singing his favorite song, which went *Do do do*. His forefingers were extended and he was preparing to give Sean and Jack a welcoming D D D when Jack said, "Monst, people have been saying that you and I are the same!"

"The same?" said the Monst.

"Yes, the same. It's a rumor that's been going around. Why, even Sean here—"

"You think I'm Jack?" said the Monster to Sean.

"Not exactly," said Sean, "I think Jack is you."

"Oh," said the Monster, somewhat puzzled by this.

"I think Jack *plays* you," said Sean.

"Jack plays me?" said the Monster. "I thought he played the guitar."

"Yes, he does play the guitar," answered Sean patiently.

"THE MONST"

"But he also plays *you*."

"Do I *sound* like the guitar?" asked the Monster, who was beginning to get very perplexed.

"No, not much," Sean admitted. "I mean Jack plays you the way an actor plays a role."

They had had rolls for breakfast that morning so the Monster was naturally a little confused by Sean's turn of phrase. "I thought Jack *ate* his rolls this morning."

"Yes, he did," said Sean.

"You should *never* play with your food," said the Monster seriously.

"No," said Sean. "No, you shouldn't. Monster, you're a *part* Jack plays."

"I'm apart?" said the Monster. "No, I'm right here."

"*Mon*ster!" said Sean, exasperated. "*You don't exist!*"

"Huh?" said the D D D Monster.

"You see," said Jack, "it's perfectly clear that we're separate people. It's as plain as the nose on your face. How could anyone make that mistake?"

"Oh, all right," said Sean, tired. It had been a long day at school. "All right, you're separate people."

"I'm Jack!" said the Monster.

"What?" said Sean.

"I'm Jack!" the Monster repeated. "*Do do do. Do do do.*"

"This is a very strange family," said Sean.

"Yes," said the Monster. "But it's a *nice* family."

"Nice, but strange," thought Sean. "In fact—"

"Sean," said the Monster, "is there anything you might like to say to me?"

Sean was at the end of his tether. He was really tired. He gave in. "*Shut up, D,*" he said wearily.

"Thank you, Sean," said the Monster, smiling. And he immediately shut up.

"Let's say mean things about Jack," said the Monster.

"All right," said the Astronaut.

But the Monster couldn't think of a single mean thing to say.

"Monster," said the Astronaut, "you're pitiful."

"*Thank* you," said the Monster.

"Shut up, D," said the Astronaut, smiling on a sunshiny day.

The Monster smiled back. As usual, he began to talk.

Coda: Le Monstre Bien-Rangé

Un jour, le monstre a décidé de visiter son grand ami de vingt ans, Ravi. Il a voyagé à la France, où Ravi demeurait. En France le monste est un peu renommé. Il est "le plus grand monstre de D D D de la France (aussi le seul)."

Le monst était étonné de decouvrir que Ravi n'était plus enfant. Ravi est homme: il s'était marié à une très belle jeune fille qui s'appellait Christelle. ("Elle est comme cristal," pensait le monst.) Et Ravi et Christelle étaient les fiers parents de Léna, une belle enfante de presque deux ans. "Par ma barbe," pensait le monst, "comme le têmps coule! Les enfants deviennent les parents—et voilà! plus d'enfants." Mais le monst—le monst est toujours le monst, ni homme ni parent ni enfant. Ca c'est très mystèrieux pour la pauvre créature. Alors, il est "le plus grand," mais personne ne le connaît. Est-il monstreux, ce monstre? Non. Il est ni homme ni bête. En vérité, c'était bizarre. Mais Ravi—grand ami du monst—a dit, "Ça va, Monst. Ça va. Ca n'est pas grande chose. Tu es le monst. Tu fais le D D D. Tu es heureux." "Heureux?" a dit le monst. "Je suis heureux?" "Mais oui," a dit Ravi avec un beau sourire. "Mais oui!" a dit le monst. C'était vrai. Il était heureux. "Quelle visite!" a dit le monstre. Et il a donné un grand D D D à son ami français.

The Well-Brought-Up Monster

One day, the Monst decided to visit his great friend of twenty years, Ravi. He traveled to France, where Ravi lived. In France the monster is a little bit known. He is "the greatest Monster of DDD of France (also the only one)."

The Monst was astonished to discover that Ravi was no longer a child. Ravi is a man: he married a very beautiful young woman named Christelle. ("She is like crystal," thought the Monst.) And Ravi and Christelle were the proud parents of Lena, a beautiful child of nearly two years. "By my beard," thought the Monst (whose command of idiomatic French was a bit out of date), "how time runs on! Children become parents—and then more children." But the Monst—the Monst is always the Monst, neither man nor parent nor child. That was very mysterious to the poor creature. He is "the greatest," but no one knows him. Is he monstrous, this monster? No. He is neither man nor beast. In truth, it was bizarre. But Ravi—the Monst's great friend—said, "It's all right, Monst. It's all right. It's no big thing. You are the Monst. You go D D D. You are happy." "Happy?" said the Monst. "I'm happy?" "Yes!" said Ravi with a beautiful smile. "Yes!" said the Monst. It was true. He was happy. "What a visit!" said the monster. And he gave a big D D D to his French friend.

The Ern Malley Story

Do you know about Ern Malley? Do you know that story? I'll tell you.

It was i'""""""""""""""""""""""""""""""""""""""'n Australia, during the war, the middle 40s. Australia, you know was always a bit of a backwater. It was never much for the Modernist sort of literature but it had one you know *little* magazine the kind which prints incomprehensible material and everyone loves it. It was called *Angry Penguins. Angrrrrrrrrrrrry Penguinnnnnnnnnnns.* Its editor was Max Harris, and he was charismatic and indefatigable and argumentative. There were people who loved Max Harris. There were people who hated him. Once a group of these latter got together and tossed him in the river. The river was called The Torrens and it was a sunlit winter's day in 1941. But he was none the worse for it. Max Harris was bringing Modernism to Australia with a vengeance, you know, T.S.E., Dylan Thomas, modernism. And Max Harris was a fearsome Moderrrrrrrrrrrrrrrrrrrrrn poet himself. He was a young man, really, in his 20s, and full of energy.

Oh, but there were others who had energy too. They say when you hated people in those days you *really* hated them. The war was on and so there was an official enemy to hate. But whom could one hate at home? Two young men in the army, also in their 20s, hated Max Harris and they hated Modernism. Their names were Harold Stewart and James McAuley. It was a Saturday afternoon in early October 1943.

Lieutenant James McAuley and Corporal Harold Stewart were at their desks in the general office of L Block at the Victoria Barracks. They were the rostered CO and NCO on duty at their outfit, the Directorate of Research and Civil Affairs. The barracks...is a handsome, Georgian-style bluestone building, fronted by lawn, palms and ornamental cannon on St. Kilda Road, the leafy boulevard that sweeps from the south-east across the Yarra River into the city—but L Block, a little to the west of the main building, was a scruffy old weatherboard shed with a tin roof.[2]

Stewart and McAuley decided to play a marvelous joke. They decided they would invent a poet, a *modernist* poet, and they would call him Ern Malley. They would say that Ern Malley died young, like Keats, but that he had a sister Ethel who had discovered some of his poetry after his death. Ethel of course couldn't pretend to judge her brother's poetry, but she was sending a sample to Max Harris to find out if it had any merit.

Amid great hilarity, and in very little time, McCauley and Stewart produced a sheaf of poems—enough for a small book—and they sent some to Max Harris.

Max Harris fell for it hook line and sinker. Poor Ern, the hoaxers told him through the medium of Ethel, was

---

[2] Passages in italics are from Michael Heyward, *The Ern Malley Affair* (London: Faber and Faber, Limited, 1993). All typos intended.

a garage mechanic. He had never show his poetry to anyone. Was it any good? Here is one of the poems they sent:

Dürer: Innsbruck, 1495

> I had often, cowled in the slumberous heavy air,
> Closed my inanimate lids to find it real,
> As I knew it would be, the colourful spires
> And painted roofs, the high snows glimpsed at the back,
> All reversed in the quiet reflecting waters—
> Not knowing then that Dürer perceived it too.
> Now I find that once more I have shrunk
> To an interloper, robber of dead men's dream,
> I had read in books that art is not easy
> But no one warned that the mind repeats
> In its ignorance the vision of others. I am still
> The black swan of trespass on alien waters.

Is it good? Max Harris thought it was very good. Here at last was an Australian modernist. The backwater had finally joined the 20th Century. True, the young man had died. But the tragedy of his death was mitigated by the fact that here, preserved, was a slim volume of his work, appropriately titled *The Darkening Ecliptic.* A special issue of the magazine was prepared and published.

Then the news broke. It was all over the newspapers.

Modernism in Australia has never been the same. Of course it has never been the same anywhere else either.

But the hoaxers were by no means the winners in all this. They had the first, not the last laugh. It has been pointed out that the poetry written by Harold Stewart and James McCauley as Ern Malley was *better* than anything they published under their own names. Were the deceivers themselves deceived? Is it possible that by parodying the modern idiom they were worked upon by the same forces which *produced* the modern idiom? Zeitgeist flashes in funny ways and chooseth whom it will.

In the mid-seventies, at Brooklyn College, John Ashbery would, in the exam for the creative writing course he taught, print without attribution one of Geoffrey Hill's Mercian Hymns... *beside a poem by Ern Malley, and tell his students: "One of the two poems below is by a highly respected contemporary poet; the other is a hoax originally published to spoof the obscurity of much modern poetry. Which do you think is which? Give your reasons."*

As Michael Heyward tells us:

The hoax is the most fascinating thing Angry Penguins *ever published. In cooking up their poet to a satirical recipe, McAuley and Stewart threw into the brew a seasoning of anarchic intelligence and comic self-laceration. Writing pretentiously, they described a mind so aware of pretension that it debunks itself with aplomb. In the end, Malley is really unlike the sort of grandstanding, romantic surrealism he mocks. It pays to remember that two very different temperaments and personalities were constructing the work without bothering to smooth the edges. Like a medium possessed by a host of spirits, Ern Malley freely exhibits his multiple consciousness. There is not one Ern Malley but several, and they are all mutually exclusive characters. There is Ern Malley,*

THE ERN MALLEY STORY

the black swan of trespass, the native modernist talented enough to turn the poetic tradition of his country on its head. There is Ern Malley the jejune and modish experimentalist who does belly-flops in his attempt to look significant. There is the Ern Malley who bravely stares his own death in the face, and the Ern Malley who slyly tells the reader he never was. All these writers were essential to the hoaxers' fiction. Each contradicts the others and helps give the poetry its dizzy, speeded-up quality, as Malley rifles through his composite self.

Ern Malley may never have existed, but, at this point, like the "real" Keats, he is nothing but literature. And literature is notoriously free. It can mean anything. *Which do you think is which? Give your reasons.*

Ern Malley writes,

> There is a moment when the pelvis
> Explodes like a grenade. I
> Who have lived in the shadow that each act
> Casts on the next act now emerge
> As loyal as the thistle that in session
> Puffs its full seed upon the indicative air.
> I have split the infinitive. Beyond is anything.

The Tiger and Other Tales

Families

We think sometimes that things will always stay the same. Sometimes we want them to change. Sometimes we want them to stay the same. But no matter what we want, things change.

The family is like that. It has changed too. In the old days, if someone did you an injury you would not go to the police, as you would today. You would go to your brother or perhaps your father or an influential relative. They would do what needed to be done and not the police. The police were weak, in a way. The family was strong. But the family was not just yourself and your mother and your father. The family was yourself and your mother and your father and your grandmothers and your grandfathers and all your relatives too.

With the discovery of the New World, the discovery of America, something very important happened to the family. Can you imagine what it was like to cross the ocean in those days? It was a crossing which was full of danger and peril and the fear of disease. It must have been like a journey through space to another planet. While it was true that many members of your family might journey with you, it was also true that many would stay behind, content to remain in the old world, where they had been for generations. The new world was full of interest and change and hope.

Now, there is something about America which it is always important to remember whenever you think about it, or whenever you want to know what it means to be an American. That is the size of America. America is, almost, as big a place as can be imagined. Its vast area extends from one ocean to another and the spaces in between have places in them so different from one another that you cannot help but think that the people living there must be different too. This size of America is a very important thing. For many years in America—though perhaps not today—it was always possible to find a new place, always possible to make a perilous journey through a wilderness in the hope of finding a new world within the new world.

And families did go away. It was no longer necessary to be protected by your father or your brother, or perhaps an influential uncle or aunt. The police were there to do that, and they were very strong in the new world. But what if a person disliked his family? Could he change that too? It was discovered in America, though it had been discovered in the old world too, that it was possible to CHANGE THE FAMILY, that the family could become something new and different from what it was. Nowadays we see families living with no relatives near-by, we see families which are a mother and child living together and

FAMILIES

a father living somewhere else, or a father and child living together and a mother living somewhere else. We see all these things because we *live in America*, in the new world, in a place in which we can always say that some people in our families, many years ago, decided that they would no longer live in the way that generations had lived before them, that they would take new hope upon themselves,

    and journey forth.

> "we got the schoolhouse blues
> the schoolhouse blues
> tired of reading history
> don't care for geography
> we're getting oh so sick
> of doin our arithmetic
> that's why
> we gave the teacher the sack
> and
> we're never gonna go back
> if she doesn't like it she can SIT ON A TACK
> we got the
>   schoolhouse
>   blues"
>
>   —Irving Berlin (1922)

The Tiger and Other Tales

Harry Fox (Dead) To George M. Cohan (Dead)

(The dead Cohan has just sent the dead Fox a birthday card)

Dear Georgie,

Gee, it's good to hear from you—especially being that you've been dead for over sixty years. You know how a good word will cheer a fella when he's a little down, and after all not everybody even remembers birthdays. To get a birthday card from a corpse is something really special, and I'm telling you I'll never forget it.

How is it out there, Georgie? You know, us Catholics, we get told a lot of things and I guess they're all true, but you're the one who used to sing, "Hurried and worried until we're buried, and there's no curtain call." You remember that, Georgie? Right up to the footlights you'd go and you gave it all you had. I remember those days, Georgie. How you used to put that leg of yours way up on the proscenium wall and then you'd jump. Oh, you was something, Georgie, you was something. I don't know much about heaven or—that other place, or wherever we might end up, but, Georgie, I hope you still got your dancing shoes. And I remember the Four Cohans, and oh, what a dancer that Josie was. And Jerry—there was a song and dance man, a *really good* song and dance man. Oh, and Nellie with that big smile of hers. Whatever happens to people, Georgie? They flash, you know, right out at you as if they was some big piece of the sun and then they're gone.

But they're not forgotten, Georgie, no they're not, not as long as I'm here. I was never much, you remember, but you always thought I did a pretty good Essence just like old Prim with his blarney, and I could sing on key. Is it the Irish, Georgie? Do they flash out at you more than others? Or was it just that time, a time that made room for people to be—to be people. Nora Bayes, she wasn't Irish, Georgie but you let her introduce "Over There." And Sam, your partner, what a guy he was. And what a guy you were. That doesn't die, does it Georgie? That can't just vanish, can it? Isn't that really what us Catholics believe in the end? That goodness and decency don't just vanish: that they stay always, even if you drive nails in them and put them on a cross you can't kill them. Goodness don't die, Georgie, any more than you did. This card is proof of that. Some people sing from the larynx, and they sing ok, but if you sing from the heart (even if it goes through your nose) you make something. And it stays.

You know, Georgie, it occurs to me that I must be dead, too. How can I remember all that stuff from a hundred years ago and still be alive? I must be dead, Georgie. But it isn't anything I notice too strongly. You could have sent me a deathday card, Georgie, you could have done that.

HARRY FOX (DEAD) TO GEORGE M. COHAN (DEAD)

Maybe you even know the day I died, which is more than I do. But, Georgie, you didn't, you sent me a birthday card, remembering when I first came into the world. Where do we come from? Who knows, but we're here and at least some of us shine for a little while. I'm more shadow than shining, Georgie, but you remembered me and you sent your regards. I won't forget it, Georgie, not as long as I'm dead.

And that's the kind of little guys we are.

Harry

The Tiger and Other Tales

BROUGHTON FOUNTAIN

For James Broughton

The Master stood on the edge of the cliff. He asked which of his disciples would thrust himself over the side, plunging into the mouth of a horrible and certain death. "I," said one, eager to get a running start.

"Wait," said the Master. "Do you think I'm some sort of idiot? I was only raising an abstract question. I need all the disciples I can get—and besides, it's a long way down the side of that cliff." "True," said the eager disciple. "But wouldn't you always honor the name of the disciple who *died* for you?" "Well, I might," said the Master, "but really it all depends on whether I've written it down. My memory's a little shaky these days, and I can't seem to locate my pencil."

"Master," said the disciple, "*I* would be the one who *died* for you!" "Well, go ahead if you must," said the Master, fumbling in his pockets for a piece of paper. "But I'm not guaranteeing anything. Oh, where is that pencil!" "*Thank you*, Master. Aieeeee!" said the disciple as he leaped over the edge. "What *was* his name?" said the Master. "I suppose," said another disciple, "there isn't much left of him now."

The disciples looked at each other silently. The wind sprang up. They were suddenly filled with a strange ecstasy. "Aieeeee," they began to say, "aieeeee, aieeeee," and made for the edge of the cliff. "Hey, wait a minute," said the Master, "whose disciples are you anyway, mine or his?" "Why, yours, of course," said the disciples, stopping in their tracks. "That's better," said the Master. "You should at least look before you leap. It's been a rather bad year for disciples, you know, and I'd just as soon have you stay a—" But before the Master was able to say the word "live," the disciple who had leapt over the cliff suddenly appeared in front of him, looking only a little the worse for wear.

"Aieeeee," said the Master, "what are *you* doing here?" "I'm *back*," said the disciple. "Death really isn't all it's cracked up to be." "You—died?" said the Master. "Yes," said the disciple. "But what was it like?" "Not too bad, you know, nothing much really. A bit of a splat at the bottom. Otherwise fit as a fiddle actually." "But you've seen what no one else has ever seen and come back to talk of." "Well, yes, I suppose I have." "Won't you tell us about it?" "Well, all right. I saw—"

But at this point a strong wind suddenly sprang up and lifted the seemingly solid body of the disciple up into the air like a leaf. His body seemed to collapse upon itself, to fold inward, to become nothing, nothing but a piece of scattered debris upon the wind. "Master," came the cry,

"Master, Master—" Then nothing.

"He must have had a name," said the Master. "Perhaps it was James. That certainly was a strong wind!" "Master," said another disciple, "could we leave this place?" "Yes, yes," said the Master, "I'm not enjoying it very much myself. Let's go." But then they realized that it was night and they *couldn't* go. They couldn't descend the mountain in darkness. "Oh, Fudge," said the Master as another burst of wind took his hat over the side of the cliff. "I was very fond of that hat too."

"Fonder than you were of me, I sometimes think," came the voice. It was James. "Good lord, you're back again." "Yes," said James, "you know, it's better the second time around. The first time you have problems with that *awful* dog." "Did you get bitten?" "Not the second time!" "But James, how do you manage it?—dying and resurrecting, dying and resurrecting." "Don't know, really. I suppose it's just a sort of talent." "Indeed. Can you make my hat come back?" "Doubt it. I'll try. Mmmmph, mmmmph, nothing much there." "You can only resurrect... yourself?" "Well, now, I don't know. It is possible..." "What?" "It is possible... You now, Master, I had a terrible childhood." "What has that got to do with it?" "Beatings, always complaints—ah, here I go again!"

The wind sprang up and James was off again into the night. "What stars, Master," he said. "What stars! I wish I could take you with me. It's *wonderful* here!" It was morning now. As the Master looked around him he saw that his disciples had all vanished. There was nothing there but the mountain and the sky. He opened his mouth and began to speak:

> My name is James Richard Broughton. I was born in the valley town of Modesto on November 10, 1913. I come from a place of indescribable sweetness.

The wind sprang up again. "Master," said James, "we have the same name. Come! Come!" The Master looked up. His body seemed at once solid and—*light*. "This is It," he thought, "This is really It." "*Now*," said James, holding out his hand to the Master, "*now*." A shock of electricity shuddered between them. "IS NOW THIS IT HERE?" said the Master, "I'm *fly-ing*!" And he was.

"You see," said James, "there is no death, nothing to it." "I see," said James, "there isn't even this mountain." "Certainly not this mountain," said James. "There is something, though." "What is it?" "How can I put it? Night and day, day and night—I sound like an old song. *The indescribable sweetness of being alive!*"

They reeled through the air, covering distance upon distance. Finally they lit down on a tiny island off the coast of Asia. "We are one, Master," said James, "we have fused." "Yes," said James, "it's true. I can't tell us apart anymore." "We are Master and Disciple, Master, Disciple and Master. We are moth and flame. *We are one*. WONDROUS THE

BROUGHTON FOUNTAIN

MERGE!" "But what about *us*?" came a voice. "Yes," said another, "what about us?" "Oh, *them*," said the Master. It was all the *other* disciples hovering in the air. "I'm afraid you will have to find your own mountains," said James[2]. "We can't find them for you. It's been a very complicated life we've had to lead. Follow your bliss!"

The two James Richards waved to the creatures in the air. "Poor things," they thought, "poor sweetings. We would give them blood if we could." It was dawn again. Master and Disciple shivered a little in the chill as the sun at last came up. "Camera!" said James, "Lights! I love the movies!"

—My name is James.

There is nothing

But the indestructible   sweetness

Of

Everything! *Follow your weird.*

The Tiger and Other Tales

My Death

by David Bromige

Krishna & Ron are so very sorry. Ron met me 41 years ago (I gave a reading at the Albany Public Library with Harvey Bialy which Ron attended) and I was a wonderful & generous friend the entire time. David, "sturdy"—like a rock or a tree... Stephen heard me read in the city in the mid 80s, wrote "Cracking the Code" for The Difficulties issue devoted to my work. Charles Bernstein loved me and my work and my death fills him with sorrow. William Knight is very sorry to hear of my passing. He met me on several of my visits to Vancouver to see Chris and to do readings. He remembers the quicksilver, the knife edge, the words that softly split his head open. And laughing with me later. Steve Tills just learned of this a minute ago—has been busy moving to a new home. Aside from his own father, I was pretty much the dearest and most generous man Steve will ever know. He will miss me like the dickens. I taught them all how to be alive and how to squeeze everything meaningful and fun and loving and real out of every moment we live. Gosh, he loves me. For Charles Bernstein, I was a prince of poetry and a wonderful friend and compatriot. "A Great Companion," as Robin Blaser said. Curtis Faville didn't know me but his wife took her first English course at Berkeley from me when I was still a TA in the Department there, pursuing my graduate degree. I was a juvenile diabetic, but lived to be 75. This alone is a feat almost beyond belief. He is sorry he never had the occasion to know me. George Bowering will always remember the poem I wrote in the cafeteria at UBC: "Borrowing from Bowering / is a neat / feat." He just turned his tired old neck to the left and saw his shelf of Bromide books, and said thank goodness, and in his head I scoffed at the object of that verb. D.A. Powell said I was his first teacher. What one of us lacked, the other forgave. Tom Raworth said I will be missed. It's a clear dawn there on the South Coast of England: sunlight on cream-painted Regency houses he looks past to arrive at the sea. And the light reminds him of the last time he spent with me, some years ago, when I drove him from Santa Rosa over to Camp Meeker where Val, the children and he had lived back in the seventies. He remembers the echo of our tread on the boardwalk of Occidental Fragments of memory. Ed Coletti says it rained untimely this morning early on in June when I disappeared.

An E-mail to George

It was right after my brother's death. My friends noticed how depressed I was, and they tried to cheer me up. One of them said, "I don't know how much you believe in the 'other world,' but, you know, I understand there's a special *psychic* web site. I never visited it myself, but people say it's, well, fun. Maybe there's something to it, maybe you could get a message through to George, tell him you miss him."

I scoffed of course, but my friend gave me the URL so I looked it up. It was

```
http://www.dead.off
```

There wasn't much on the site. It had a stylized cypress tree and the words *D*elivery of *E*-mail to the *A*bsent and *D*eceased: *DEAD*.

I wrote "George" in the search engine box. "Insufficient data" came back. I tried with two names: George Mortis. This time, bingo! George Hamilton Mortis—my brother! Dear George, I wrote,

```
How is it with you? I miss you a lot. You
would have enjoyed your funeral. Old
Ms. Prentice actually cried. I wish you were
here.

Your brother,

Jack
```

I pressed the send button. Nothing happened, so I closed the system down.

The next day I went online again. My in-box had a message from `GHM@dead.off`. My God, I thought.

> Hi Jack,
>
> Nice to hear from you, especially under these circumstances. Being dead isn't that different from being alive. I see all the guys who croaked, and they all send their regards, Jerry especially. Mom and Dad have a nice little set-up: they even have servants, which they never did when they were alive.
>
> I miss you too, but I'm busy busy busy. They heard I was good at numbers, so they have me going through their books. You wouldn't believe the centuries of errors! People who were supposed to be alive, dead; people who were supposed to be dead, alive. A real nightmare.
>
> Well, gotta fly. I can't exactly say I wish you were here, but i sure wish I could see you, Bud. Sometimes if I just close my eyes, I think I can.
>
> Your brother,
>
> George

My dead brother sending me an e-mail! It seemed insane. Surely it was some sort of joke—in terrible taste! Someone who knew me and knew George was having the time of his life over this. But who could it be? And who would know that George called me "Bud"? He never did that in public. It was just when we were alone. "Bud," he'd say, "you're my buddy, right." "Right," I'd say, "always there for you." Bud. Who would know about that?

On Sunday, after the service, I asked Father Kevin, the priest at St. Joseph's, if I could speak with him.

"What is it, my son?" said the priest.

"Father," I said, "I've been talking to my brother."

"Now, Jack, your brother is dead."

"Yes, he is. But I've been talking to him."

The priest waited a beat. "How long has this been going on?" he asked.

"Not long. Just since Friday."

"Well, it's natural," he said, "when we miss somebody, to pretend to ourselves that he's still here. Sometimes we get a little carried away and think he actually is."

"I'm not pretending, Father. I write him e-mail."

"You write him e-mail?"

"Yes."

"And he answers?"

"Yes."

"What does he say?"

"Not too much. He says he's busy over there. He says it's not too different from being here."

"Jack, would you consider psychological help for this problem of yours? I know a good therapist. Catholic, not too expensive."

"Father, I know it sounds crazy. I wouldn't believe it myself, only George had a special name for me; I don't think anybody knew this name, and, Father, the name was in the e-mail."

"The name was in the e-mail?"

"I swear by all the saints, father. It's a name only he and I knew. And it's in the e-mail. You have to go to a special web site to access this place."

"Can anyone go to this web site?"

"I don't see why not."

The priest took me into his study. He logged onto the site and typed in my brother's name. This time a reply came immediately.

"*Get that goddamn serpent in skirts away from me!*" said the e-mail.

"What?" said the astonished priest.

"*He is an abomination before the Lord, a two-faced jackal. Ah, Bud, help me! Help me! The Suffering—*"

"Is this some kind of joke?" said the priest angrily.

"No, Father, I swear. I'm as surprised as you."

He looked again at the message. "*The Suffering—* Did your brother receive last rites?"

"Yes, Father, he did. What could he have meant by 'The Suffering'? And why would he have attacked you like

AN E-MAIL TO GEORGE

that?" I felt suddenly cold, extremely cold. "Could George be in a situation of" (I couldn't think of another word) "damnation? Oh, God!"

"I need to speak to my superiors," said Father Kevin. "First, let's print this out. We need to find out more about this so-called 'web-site.'"

I left him there and went home, shaken.

When I entered the house, the phone was ringing. It was Hank, the friend who first told me about the web site.

"Hi, Jack," he said. "I just wanted to apologize for telling you about that web-site."

"Apologize?"

"Yes, yes. It's totally phoney. You didn't contact them, did you?"

"Well, yes, I did."

"It's a total set-up. They get you going with all your grief and get your hopes up and then they ask you for money. It's only for the gullible."

"Gullible?"

"Yes, it's a scam. There's an article in today's *Chronicle*. Page 25A."

I looked and he was right. There it was in print. "INTERNET SCAM FEEDS ON GRIEF."

"You didn't give them any money did you?" he asked.

"No, no money."

"I'm sorry. I thought it was for real."

"Thanks, Hank."

I hung up the phone and tried to find the site. No luck. I supposed it had been shut down. I phoned Father Kevin to tell him this latest development. "Ah," he said, "so that's it. Poor gullible people! We found out just in time."

"Yes, Father, I guess we did."

"You know, Jack, God is not mocked," said the priest.

"God is not mocked," I answered.

"He protects us even in our moments of weakness and vulnerability."

The next morning there was a message in my in-box. It was from `GHM@dead.off`.

```
Hey, Bro,
How ya doin man. Wow, it's ok here.
Do you remember Ms. Peters, our sixth-grade
teacher? She says hello. She's been here for
years. Still looks the same. And Annie
Ruffner? What a body she had. Not now,
though.
Hey, gotta go.
Keep your pecker up, buddy.
```

It went on like this for days—messages of the most unspeakable banality. Worse: I couldn't even reply to them. The site had completely disappeared. I read the messages over and over and thought: My brother had a better side than this. He could be like this, yes. But there was also an enthusiasm, a genuine intellectual excitement. That was

AN E-MAIL TO GEORGE

missing here. How could he go on and on in this way? Nothing but banalities day after day. How could *I* go on?

And then something happened. It began to occur to me that I hated my brother, really hated him. Couldn't stand the sight of him. I had forgotten all about that in the disaster of his death—brought on by his own bad driving, the fool! He was stupid, stupid, going out that night in the rain, and drinking. "I'll be fine," he laughed. Fine was he! Crashing into a tree as he was going sixty miles an hour in a forty mile an hour zone on a stormy night, with the rain pelting him. Fine indeed. They oughta keep those trees from moving around ha ha! Head through the window, crash. Not even wearing his seat belt. My brother the know-it-all, certain of everything. Nothing could happen to *him* could it. And now, see what happened. You're dead, that's what happened. You're dead and you've left me and I don't know what to do without you. And now your ghost your goddamn ghost is come back and it's not even really you it's just this terrible e-mail. To be haunted by a communications device! And maybe I'm not haunted at all. Maybe part of me is typing it out while the other part isn't looking—maybe it's all me. That would be just like you, just like you, haunting me but making me do all the work. What a bastard you are, and always were.

And it occurred to me that I *hated* my brother. Not merely disliked him, hated him, hated him all my life and never knew it. Could never admit it. Always so superior.

Always so holier than thou. Always so "intelligent." Not intelligent enough to know that you shouldn't drink and drive, you ninny! Wham into that tree! You bastard...Tears of rage and fury shook my entire body.

And then I saw that my in-box had a new message, something I hadn't seen before. It was dated only a minute or two ago. It was from—who else?—my brother. It said,

> You are taking on my suffering. Thank you. I could stand it no longer and felt an opening to you and you opened and took it upon you, and I am relieved. Thank you, thank you. The tears in my eyes are tears of gratitude, which I will feel for all eternity. My pain was nearly unbearable, and you have lessened it. Thank you, thank you.

As I read the message, I began to weep once more. Would I never see him again? Would my own death be like his? I remembered the innumerable ways in which our lives had touched. Since childhood, and as we became adults together. And then his death and how shattered I was. Never to hear him enter a room again. Never to hear his voice.

I felt a flush of love for the dear, dear man he was and for our time together. I highlighted the message.

And I pushed *Delete*.

Malèna

Dearest Señora Malèna,

You understand that it is particularly difficult for me to write this letter since I am not only a child but a fictional one—one appearing in a film. But, after all, you are a fictional character too, though not a child. To tell you the truth, I have been watching you for years. This is no strange thing, since everyone in this town watches you all the time. But I am the one who stole your black panties. I hope it did not inconvenience you too greatly. Such beautiful things must be scarce in wartime, especially when one's country is *losing* the war. Your great beauty inspires me daily.

Most of the men who see you want to go to bed with you. I am no exception to this rule. When my father brought me to a brothel, I chose a whore who looked like you. (I do not mean to imply that the whore resembled you in any other way.) However, I think that my feelings are not limited to the sexual. You may have heard, when I briefly went mad, I recited poetry. I think I must believe in the soul. Perhaps I confuse you with my soul. For a child, the world of adults—and, for me, the world of war—is like a movie I watch, just as I watch you. I see it going on and I am even touched by it, but I can't influence it. It ignores me. I hope you will forgive me for saying that your life, though undoubtedly real to you, was a kind of movie to me. I can't express to you the pain I felt when I saw you beaten by those horrible women. Yet what could I do? Only watch.

Had you seen me—which you did not—you would have seen me grow or struggle to grow out of my childhood. I got my first pair of long pants. My father brought me to a whore, who was the first woman ever to make love to me. The significance of such moments was not as great as I hoped it would be. Twice, though, it was permitted to me to touch you, in a small way. Once, I wrote a note to your husband. (I wrote many notes and poems to you but could not deliver them.) And once I helped you pick up some oranges you had dropped. These were, for me, my first real passage into adulthood, not my long pants or my first sexual experience: these were the moments when I realized I could do something, however small, to help another person. This, oddly enough, was my entrance into manhood. It was also the moment when I stepped out of the movie—or, more accurately perhaps, into it.

I wish I could return your black panties to you. Unfortunately, my father discovered them adorning my forehead and my mother subsequently burned them in disgust. I hope you will not think it crude of me to say that I know another who sometimes wears black panties. You were my first love. You were also the first person I could truly help. How memorable that makes you. Perhaps your

MALÈNA

beauty has faded, though I doubt it. Perhaps you have begun to forget the events that happened to you in our town. It was not a bad town, though some very bad things happened in it. For me, it was the place in which love, finding some very unlikely tinder, burst into flame.

Yours Sincerely,

Renato Amoroso

The Tiger and Other Tales

Man Wolf

a tale to keep you awake

"*Homo homini lupus.*"

There was a man who was a man for
four days of the week. On the other
three days he was a wolf. When he was a man,
he led a man's life, behaving as
other men do. But when he was a wolf
he behaved as a wolf. On
those days he retreated to a near-by
wood and, throwing his clothes off,
he feasted on whatever he could find there.
Once he discovered there was a mouse
in his house. Man
set a trap but to no avail.
On Thursday
wolf found the mouse and feasted.
Man had a wife
who was devoted
but who wondered
where he might be on
Thursday, Friday, and Saturday.

The Tiger and Other Tales

Does he have a mistress,
she wondered.
He was a good husband
and provided for her well
but his absences
filled her with foreboding.
He told her he had
business on those days
but she wondered why he would
return on Sunday wearing the same
clothing he had worn on Thursday—
and why it was not soiled but appeared to
have been unused.
Was he naked on those days?
Did he put on another skin?
Man made love to her
in a man's way, but she could feel
a certain restraint, a certain violence
that was restrained, a certain fierceness
underneath. The fierceness
excited her but scared her too.
"What do you do on those days?"
she asked him, but he would say
only this: "Business,
I told you, I have business."
But she asked him again, and finally he told her.

MAN WOLF

"*Garwaf*," he said,
"But the key is clothing."
He had never told anyone.
It excited him to tell her.
"When I am man
I wear man's clothing,
but when I am wolf
I discard my clothes.
When I put the clothes back on
I return to man."
The woman realized
she had never seen him naked,
even when they made love.
Had he been naked,
he would have been
Animal.
She wasn't sure she believed him
but she feared
Animal.
"Oh, my dear," she said,
"how interesting this is.
how my admiration for you
grows."
"It is a relief to tell you," he said.

The Tiger and Other Tales

"*Garwaf*," she said
and kissed his face.
The next day he was in the woods.

"But, my dear," the wife said,
"you must hide your
precious clothing somewhere.
You must take care.
If someone stole it
you could not return to man."
"I have a special place," he said.
"On the edge of the forest
there is a large gray rock.
Beneath it is a pit.
It's there that I place my clothing.
It is safe because no one thinks
to move the rock."
"Oh, how clever," said the woman,
"I should have known you would find
a perfect place.
Will you show it to me?"
"I don't know that I should," said the man.
"You can trust me," said the wife,
"In the fury of wolf, you might forget one day
where you have placed your clothing.

MAN WOLF

I could find it for you."
"That's true," said the man
and showed her the place, the rock, the pit.

The woman telephoned her lover,
saying, "You will not believe this,"
and told him the story of the man who was a wolf.
"But the key is clothing,"
she said. "If we steal his clothing,
he will not be able to come back as man."
So the woman and her lover
found the rock, the pit, and took the clothing.
And the man as wolf came back to the rock
and found nothing
and knew he had been deceived.
But he was naked
and could not return.
He was wolf only.
His howl—
pitiable and terrifying—
filled the woods for hours.
The woman and her lover,
delighted by their success,
took the man's lands
his clothes

his food
his pipe
his books and newspapers,
and lived as man and wife.
Naked, they made love.
The lover
wore the man's socks and slippers,
he sported his shirts and ties.

One day the king was hunting in the woods.

His hounds sensed the wolf near by
and ran for him.
Wolf bounded away but was not quick enough
and the hounds tore at his flesh.
Wolf cried out in pain,
but it was a man's voice that made the cry.
Astonished, the king bade his hounds cease.
"What are you?" he asked.
"Gracious sire," said the wolf,
"I am a wolf who was once a man,
a man wolf.
Please do not kill me.
I have been betrayed and banished to the woods,
but if you bring me to your castle
you will have no greater servant than wolf.

MAN WOLF

I will sniff out your enemies,
I will kill them,
I will protect your friends.
and I will tell you stories
of wolf life
of the free air that a wolf breathes
of the secrets
that only wolves know.
Spare me, Sire, and I will give you all my strength and all
    my love.
Ahwooooooooo."
The king was moved by the wolf's eloquent words and
    said, "Yes."
So the wolf lived with the king for many months.

Then the wife and the lover appeared before the king.
They were trying to convince the king to lower their
    taxes.
They argued that they were poor, honest people trying
    to make their way in the world.
But wolf saw them and knew who they were.
"Revenge," he cried.
Had he been man,
he might have sought legal recourse,
he might have hired a team of lawyers,

The Tiger and Other Tales

he might have brought the case to court.
But he was not man, he was wolf
and he raged as wolves raged.
The wife was first, and then the man.

They screamed as his strong teeth tore into their flesh.
Their blood spilled on the palace floor.

"Ah," said wolf.

The king was astonished because the wolf had always
    been a peaceful creature before.
But when he had finished, the wolf explained what the
    man and the woman had done to him.
The king understood.
He furnished the wolf with clothing and arranged for
    him to return to his home as man
for four days of the week, but to be wolf for three.
On the seventh day, the man prayed for the king, for
    himself, and for wolf.
As man, he kissed the king's hand; as wolf, he licked the
    king's boots.
Both man and wolf lived for many years and had many,
    many descendants.
I am one of them.
Garwaf.

This story comes from Marie de France in the 12th century. I was reading Dorothy Gilbert's translation.

The Tiger

To the memory of my friend, Michael Lurie

> There is a constant play of light and color on the bellying square sails (silver in moonlight, black in starlight, cloth-of-gold at sunset, white as the clouds themselves at noon)
> —S.E. Morrison, *Christopher Columbus, Mariner*

He was about twelve years old. Born in East Oakland. Black. Dark-brown in color. He stared for a long time at a wall in San Francisco on which was written the words, FUCK NIGGERS. Why couldn't any of us say anything about it? One of us said (later), "I realized at that time how much of a 'womb' East Oakland was."

> *the failure to attack it*
>   *to attack racism*
>   *whenever and wherever it*
>   *occurs—*

She did not wish to create a "character" or to find a "place" for that character to live. She wished to release something. Yet there were so many contrary currents within her that the release of one called to mind all the others which had *not* been released. The alternative was silence, but of course she wanted anything but silence. It was in the midst of this quandary that she encountered...(a constant play of light and color)

...

On the morning after Raguk had seen sixteen tigers leaping from the sky he awoke feeling strangely uneasy. He had of course assumed that it was a dream or an hallucination. But the tigers had been real enough. They had probably originated on Og's second moon—or so he thought as he gazed, rather stupidly as usual, up into the night sky on this one clear night in the month of Mar. One, two, three...sixteen leaping from the moon down to his own land or Ur. He had heard of such things in the ancient prophecies—*blood moon tiger child*—but he had no idea what they could have meant. Why should they suddenly appear—and why to him, a poor mekam driver? Still, how beautiful they were—leaping one after another, shimmering in that dreamlight, powerful, throbbing with all the energy of life.

"Raguk...Raguk...why are you up?"

It was his wife, Dar.

"To see the most glorious sight I have ever seen. Look."

Dar gave a slight gasp as she saw them too. One after another—glorious animals!

"Why, they're beautiful," she said. "But whyever should they come here? This—this is nowhere."

THE TIGER

"Perhaps they have come to bring us some good," said Raguk.

"What possible good could they bring?" said Dar, continuing to stare.

Now, at that moment a very odd thing happened to them, and it happened to both Raguk and Dar at the same time. They were both aware—it was not a voice but an awareness, like the sudden instantaneous solution to a problem in mathematics—of a vast benevolence which encompassed everything around them, birds trees flowers rocks sky, even themselves, the poor human creatures. It was a cry of REJOICE suddenly leaping up from the heart of things, a wild and ecstatic *clarification* of consciousness. Raguk, who understood very little of his life and who was pained by his knowledge of understanding very little, involuntarily smiled and began to sing a song he had never heard before.

"Lagoolee, lagoolee, esthur, esthur..."

He had a very bad voice and little ear for music but somehow the tune was haunting all the same.

"Rocks, barrenness," said Dar, "song is springing forth out of the barren soil. It is a miracle, Raguk."

And then—quite suddenly—there was no miracle. The tigers disappeared. Nothing was left of them, no tracks, sounds, nothing. Nothing was left but the continuous red sheen of Og's second moon.

"Raguk...where could they have gone?"

"I—don't know."

Raguk raised his hand to his brow and looked out over that night landscape. Nothing was there. Only a few shadows—rocks, boulders. But nothing alive, nothing breathing. The landscape was dead again.

"Raguk—shouldn't we…examine? Search?"

And search they did. Raguk lighted his mogore lamp and held it above his head as he scrambled among the lifeless things that stretched out for miles around his house. Nothing. Still nothing.

"Come," said Dar at last. "Come. Perhaps some sleep will help."

And so they tried to sleep. In his dreams Raguk attempted to see the creatures again but they had ceased to appear even to his dreams. He could remember nothing but the extraordinary fact of the event itself.

In the morning he awoke and felt—uneasy.

"Dar, did we—could we—"

"I don't know, Raguk."

"Dar, we must tell no one of this."

"No. Yes. No one, Raguk."

"Not even Dareena."

"Especially Dareena."

"We must think, Dar."

"Yes, Raguk. We must *think*."

But no matter how much they thought—or how hard they thought—they discovered: nothing.

THE TIGER

...

Sun-flash on the pool. My son Sean, 9, holds his head under the water to the count of six, then ten. Kicking is next. Sean in blue bathing cap, the little "black" girl next to him in red. In the crowded pool bodies "rearrange" themselves. What good is a book (she said) if no one will read it?

> all of our presidents
>   from Kennedy on
>   have been failures!
> on the loud hill
>   the wind
>   whips up from the miles
>   away!
> looking at our country
>   is like looking at a map
>   of schizophrenia!—
> streaks of cloud that frame the blue—

...

Imagine: a fat man a very fat man waddling along in what must seem to your eyes a soiled blue sheet. This is Urik, chief priest of our village. I had always avoided him even though, like everyone else, I was required to attend his services once a week. A short fat darkskinned man (I am a tall thin darkskinned man) waddling through the marketplace where I stood attending to my mekam. Sire Urik, said the ignorant populace, touch me, Sire Urik. Sire Urik, heal my disease. Even the young women. Touch me, Sire Urik. How I hated him.

"Raguk."

The sound of my own name startled me. I had no idea that Urik knew me at all. He said it again:

"Raguk!"

After a pause I answered him. Obsequiousness. "Ah, yes, Sire Urik."

"*You have seen the vision of the sixteen tigers.*"

"Wh-what?"

"*You have seen the vision of the sixteen tigers.* Do not deny it, I am certain of it anyway."

"How—how do you know, Sire Urik? Did Dar—"

"Not a word. I *know*, that's all." Urik's eyes blazed.

"But if you *know*, Sire Urik, you must know what the vision *means*. It has been an enormous burden to me. You must *tell* me, Sire Urik."

The blaze went out of his eyes.

"Unfortunately, I do not know *that*. There, unhappily, the prophecies are not clear."

"For the gods' sake, what prophecies, Sire Urik?"

"In the sixteenth chapter of the second Book of Reegam it is written that a puny and insignificant mekam driver will be granted the extraordinary vision of sixteen

THE TIGER

tigers leaping from the sky. And *then*—"

"And *then*—"

"And then, unfortunately, the text is corrupt. No one knows what 'and then' refers to."

"There are no opinions on the subject?"

"None. It is the most profoundly puzzling passage in all our scripture. Would you care to see it?"

"Of course."

"Come."

We made our way from the marketplace to the ancient temple which stood a mile away from the town. Urik signaled me to follow him inside. At the far corner of the dusty room stood an enormous bookcase. Urik sighed as he failed to reach a large blue book three shelves up. Finally he jumped into the air and pulled it down. In a moment the book was opened to the proper page. It was just as he had said. The passage began coherently enough but it ended in hopeless gibberish.

"Is there no one who can understand this?" I asked.

"No one," said Urik. "It is completely unintelligible. I was rather hoping that *you* would be able to tell *me*..."

Outside, night was beginning to fall. The red moon rose. I noticed a shaft of light pierce through the enormous windows which thrust their bulk upon every wall of the temple. I thought: The second moon is rising, covering everything with its blood.

...

"Urik, I can bear this no longer. I have begun to dream things."

"What things?"

"Fearful things. Dreadful. Also, things have begun to happen to me. Yesterday I fell down a flight of stairs. Only I didn't fall, something *tripped* me."

"You are being singled out."

"For what purpose?"

"I don't know. I can't tell you any more than that. You are being singled out. I don't know."

...

"I am not a handsome man, I am fifty years old I am cowardly and low I do not understand things as I ought I have no mission in life I am only a mekam driver (my father before me was a mekam driver his father before him was a mekam driver) I have no purpose. Urik, you must understand that nothing I have ever done or learned has in any way prepared me for this."

"None of that is relevant. You are being singled out. Do you remember Lackeem?"

"Lackeem?... Lackeem the idiot?"

"He was not an idiot. At the age of thirty-five his eyes began suddenly to cross. He tried every means at his disposal to drive them apart again. He focused one eye on

THE TIGER

one object, the other eye on another object, and then he would *move* the objects. Slowly, painfully, he would succeed in uncrossing his eyes. But the very next moment—wham!—back they were: crossed again."

"Lackeem was well known as the village idiot. Everyone thought of him as that."

"Lackeem was a saint."

"A saint? Urik, how am I to understand this? Do you remember how he drooled?"

"I used to talk to him nightly. He was on the whole less argumentative than you. He would sit upon the temple steps and say, 'Urik, I have been singled out. The gods'—but he had no idea *which* gods—'have visited me with a special affliction, I am among the chosen.'"

"And what did you say to him?"

"What could I say? I could not deny it. He had been chosen I remember him on his death bed, his long hair filthy with many years of neglect, his body soiled by his own excrement. 'Urik,' he said to me, 'Urik, I have been chosen, I have been singled out.' Even in death his eyes were crossed. Remarkable!"

"But did he never *do* anything? Urik, he must have been chosen for some purpose.

"Not necessarily, though of course there were many aspects of him of which I was ignorant. I must say that I regarded myself as the learner in this situation. It is possible that his mission was to prepare the world for *you*."

"For *me*?"

"Yes, of course. Like you he was singled out. I knew it the moment I saw you that day in the marketplace. His image flashed into my mind and I thought, "Raguk! Raguk has been chosen!""

"But my eyes aren't crossed. I'm not the village idiot. I am a mekam driver. My father was a mekam driver. That is all I am. A mekam driver."

"You are a mekam driver who has seen a vision. I knew that too."

"But did Lackeem ever refer to this vision of the sixteen tigers?"

"Not in so many words, no."

"But can't you see that my case is therefore entirely different?"

"No, not necessarily. One must allow for some latitude in these matters. It may be that you have been chosen by a god *different* from the one who chose Lackeem."

"But by *which* different god?"

"I don't know."

"And for what purpose?"

"I don't know."

...

Jesse's graduation. My arm is situated uncomfortably on the second rail of a metal railing. Downstairs I see a basketball court on which rows of chairs have been neatly

THE TIGER

arranged. Children with rifles march out. They are wearing dark green uniforms with shining silver helmets. ROTC. The military here too. The school's colors are a mismatched green—brighter than the uniforms—and gold. The gold tends towards orange, thus mismatching. There is a large sign

FREMONT

In gold on a green cloth background. The graduates march in to "Gaudiamus, Igitur." The men are in green, the women in yellow. Several wave to the audience, are applauded. Their moment of public triumph...Jesse is seventeen years old and half black, half white. When he answers the telephone he intentionally lowers his voice.

...

Raguk begins to seek out other opinions. He examines texts. Learns languages. Consults experts.

"Have you found out anything?" asks Urik.

"No, nothing."

"Have you at least remembered those words you spoke?"

"No!"

Mightn't it be a public prophecy, having to do with the health of the land? Or perhaps political? Oughtn't the king to know of this?

And so Raguk is summoned before the king.

"You don't know the meaning of this sign?"

"I do not, your Majesty!"

"Doctors, come forth to examine this man."

They do so. At last one of them steps forward.

"As far as we can determine, your Majesty, he is a perfectly normal man. A little on the stupid side, perhaps. But perfectly normal."

Raguk, who has begun to become famous, is allowed to leave. Outside, on the palace grounds, a crowd has gathered to see him. Someone says: "Stick to your guns, Raguk." Another: "Good man, Raguk!" He acknowledges them by a wave of the hand.

...

Dar walks in the metal garden.

...

Rabbi Judah said: *Nefesh* and *ruah* are conjoined, while *neshamah* has its abode in the character of a man, which place remains unknown and undiscovered. If a man strive to a pure life, he is therein assisted by holy *neshamah*, through the which he is made pure and saintly and attains to the name of holy. But if he does not strive to be righteous and pure of life, there does not animate him holy *neshamah*, but only the two grades, *nefesh* and *ruah*. More

THE TIGER

than that, he who enters into impurity is led further into it, and he is deprived of heavenly aid. Thus, each is moved forward upon the way which he takes. (*Zohar*, ed. Gershom G. Scholem)

...

he spoke quickly, as if hoping to find some other excuse for reckoning, as if, in the stiff umbrage of his circumstance, he remained somehow hopeless, unnerved, smitten, without reserve or resonance, spiteful even to the wind, which, engaged in other business (roaring) in a plain treasure, spoke slowly, groping endlessly, funneled, wretched stuff of vixen, vision, heart of the whole, heart of two minds, matters / listen / I speak / in broken / sentences / un / able to / sift one / thought from / another / in / the dark, / really. / I /
think of you and / words / hasten, break /
in the effort, break,—
shattering, the words go out—

...

Dar walks in the metal garden. Once it had been something to see. The aluminum marigolds catch the sun, like razors. The copper roses go on blossoming. Now...She remembers something. What was it, *who* was it? Her father? Someone's father? His name was Abel, Abe, Abraham, he had owned a bookstore, there was a sign on the door, Blake's *The Tyger*, an old story told her by someone, true? false? Abraham walking home, reached his house, opened the door, someone there?—

"Reality is what I mean by reality."

His friend stood before him in the uncertain light. Michael?
Yes.
They embraced. How did you—
You forgot and left the back door open again. Just as you always did. I came in, helped myself to a piece of cheese, and waited.
Bastard! Scaring the shit out of me like that. He patted his shoulder. Michael looked thin, thin. You know, you could stand sideways and no one would know you were there. You ought to have had more of that cheese, you rat!
I guess you could get me for breaking and entering.
It's funny your appearing like this. I had a dream last night of an old friend but I couldn't decide who it was. Might have been you. Anyway, I had been estranged from the friend for some reason—some petty thing. I don't know what. I said to him, We're both getting old. But he didn't answer.
Maybe he had nothing to say.
I wanted to know what it meant.
The dream?

THE TIGER

No, getting old.

It means nothing, you know. Just nothing. You get old. You die. Nothing.

I wish I could be certain even of that.

Pray for me.

I doubt that I'd know how. What an odd thing to ask.

Yes, I suppose it is. *O-r-a p-r-o n-o-b-i-s.* I'm afraid I can't stay long.

Where are you off to this time?

I don't know. Let's call it Argentina.

Argentina?

Yes. I have a situation there.

Teaching?

Yes, maybe. Learning is the real point, though. I'm tired of all this CRAP.

I thought you had tenure at L.A.

Time off for bad behavior. No one can live in L.A.

You have something permanent?

I don't know. We'll see. Anyway, I had this time in between.

Will you need a lift to the airport?

No, I have a car. A bit dented but mine. I thought I'd drop by and see you before—

Argentina's a long way off.

A lot of red meat there. Blood.

Will you try to look up Borges?

Hah—another dead man. I told you, I'm after blood.

Will a ham sandwich do?

I guess it'll have to. Whatever happened to your gourmet cooking?

Andrea got custody of the cooking. And of the politics. I lead a quiet life.

No hungry divorcees hoping for a real meal?

They'd need a real man for that. I'm tired.

You're real enough.

Maybe. You'd be surprised how much time the store takes up.

A man's work is his mistress.

I'm an old man. Anyway, where's *your* mistress?

Waiting for me in Argentina. I hope.

With dark and flashing eyes. Dances beautifully.

Probably blond and Jewish. I have a taste for contradictions. Speaking of which, my Jewish friend, where is that ham sandwich?...MMMMM, delicious. I don't know when I'll have such a sandwich again!

His friend had gone. They had embraced, exchanged good-byes. Michael had said, You know, the trouble with me is that I can only be certain I'm alive when I'm in the midst of a crisis. I manufacture them, I suppose. The words stayed in Abraham's mind: certain I'm alive. It was then that he remembered. Michael was not alive. He had been dead for several weeks. He remembered the letter, Dear Abraham, it is with great pain that we tell you... Michael had been buried in six feet of ground, he had

THE TIGER

been at the funeral himself. How could he have forgotten that? He felt a sudden tension as if his friend's spirit had leapt into his body. It was not a sensation of invasion or violation but a sudden perception of new strength, as if he had somehow merged with another and yet had remained himself. Something had happened to his mind, to his understanding over the past few hours. It had been only a few hours ago (but *had* it been a few hours?) when he had KNOWN—known with great certainty—that his friend Michael was dead, that he had been killed in an automobile accident in New York City. *He had been visited by the spirit of his dead friend.* His mind felt suddenly stretched tight, then emptied of all the constructs he had placed there with such care. His friend's spirit "walking to and fro upon the earth." What could he possibly do to relieve him of such loneliness? Dar looked out over the endless sand. I can see her now endlessly watching. Night voices whispered to her. What good is that story she asked. It belongs to another time, to another person. What good can it be for Raguk and me.

...

No. The 4 people
we do have to have.
Last though.
I don't object to.
Reviewing at budget time.

But we do need to hire them
as perm
employees
now. Turn-
over will
handle the problem

...

Various adjustments to be made between the obsessive quality of the beloved—the beloved in the head—and the actual person who can be touched, kissed.

...

Raguk opened his eyes. A horrible grayness was all around. He could not see properly. It was morning. Gray light flooded the room when he turned on the lamp. Where was Dar? Not here. He walked to the window and looked out. Nothing.

"Raguk..."

It was Dar's voice. Where was she? Outside?

He put on his coat.

"Dar...? Dar, where are you?"

Silence. Raguk could hear his own breathing.

"Dar..."

Lighting his lamp he stepped outside.

"Dar, where are you?"

THE TIGER

"Raguk..."

Dreamlight. Nothing more. Nothing more than a dream...In the midst of the dream the tiger *sprang!*

The Tiger and Other Tales

Epilogue: Two Plays

The Boy, The Girl, and the Piece of Chocolate

a ten-minute play

CHARACTERS:
THE BOY
THE GIRL

They are a "normal" upper middle-class couple in their mid thirties.

Despite the accusations, neither is particularly fat.

(The BOY appears with a box of chocolates. The GIRL, who has been seated, rises to meet him.)

BOY: Hey, we've gone through that chocolate pretty quickly.

GIRL *(Looking)*: Yes, there's only one piece left in the box.

BOY: Well, you can have it if you want.

GIRL: But it's your favorite: a truffle.

BOY: Yes, but I'd like you to have it.

GIRL: Oh, no. That's the last one. It's your favorite. It's yours.

BOY: But I'm giving it to you.

GIRL: That's a sweet gesture. But I don't need any more chocolates. I've had plenty.

BOY: Yes, I've noticed you've been gaining a little weight.

GIRL: What?

BOY: Yes, you've got a little problem with those buttons, see?

GIRL: *I* have a problem?

BOY: Yes. Only a little one. But a problem.

GIRL: You think I'm gaining weight?

BOY: I wouldn't say that exactly, but, yes, you're getting a little heftier.

GIRL: Hefty am I?

BOY: It's all right. I like big women.

GIRL: Nice of you.

BOY: And you can get even bigger by eating that piece of chocolate.

GIRL: I wouldn't touch that piece of chocolate with a ten-foot pole.

BOY: One little chocolate won't make much difference. Lots of people have a little sweet after dinner and they never show it at all.

GIRL: Maybe you think I should run around the block a

EPILOGUE: TWO PLAYS

couple of times.

BOY: Exercise never hurt anyone, you know.

GIRL: Listen, you butterball. You're fat. You've always been fat. You've been fat as long as I've known you.

BOY: Hey, this isn't about me.

GIRL: What do you mean it isn't about you. This is *all* about you. That's your chocolate.

BOY: No, no. I want you to have it.

GIRL: Why?

BOY: Because I'm nice, that's why. Because I love you.

GIRL: You want me to get fat.

BOY: I only said you had a little problem. You don't have to get so defensive.

GIRL: I'm not defensive. You're the one who needs defending.

BOY: Defensive doesn't mean needing defending.

GIRL: Who cares.

BOY: Well, I sure don't.

GIRL: Why don't we just throw the piece of chocolate away.

BOY: No, we shouldn't do that.

GIRL: Why?

BOY: It's *chocolate*.

GIRL: So?

BOY: So chocolate is special. Here, take the piece of chocolate.

GIRL: Is there poison in this piece of chocolate?

BOY: No, no, just chocolate, you know. And butter. And sugar. You know, fattening stuff.

GIRL: I'm getting tired of this talk about how fat I am.

BOY: Let's talk about something else.

GIRL: Good idea.

(Long silence)

BOY: Well, what should we talk about?

GIRL: How should I know? You're the one with all the answers.

BOY: We could talk about current events.

GIRL: I *hate* current events. Look how depressing everything is. The president, the country, everything. It's all awash in hatred and mismanagement. I hate it I hate it.

(Long silence)

BOY: How about literature?

GIRL: Bor-ing.

BOY: How about sex?

EPILOGUE: TWO PLAYS

GIRL: You mean talking about it?

BOY: I mean doing it.

GIRL: Not now, I'm not in the mood. And besides, I have a headache.

BOY: You *always* have a headache.

GIRL: I don't always have a headache. Just like a man. You expect us to be always ready. Well, we're not always ready. We have to be coaxed a little, we have to be persuaded.

BOY: That's why I was trying to give you the piece of chocolate.

GIRL: You wanted to give me the piece of chocolate so I'd give you sex?

BOY: Well, that's putting it a little bluntly, but—yes.

GIRL: You were *paying* me to give you sex?

BOY: Well, I wouldn't say "paying" you. I was giving you a piece of chocolate.

GIRL: One lousy piece of chocolate. You think that's all I'm worth?

BOY: It was my favorite kind of chocolate.

GIRL: But it was only one piece. You think I'd fuck you for one piece of chocolate.

BOY: All right, next time I'll offer two.

GIRL: I wouldn't fuck you if you offered me a hundred boxes of chocolate.

BOY: I know it. That's why I offered you only one. I don't have to offer you a lot of chocolate. All I need is one. You'll say no to that. I might as well save the rest of the box for myself.

GIRL: Yourself. That's all you think of.

BOY: Well, have you got a better subject?

GIRL: Yes, I do. I think about *the world*.

BOY: The world?

GIRL: Yes, and my place in it.

BOY: I thought you hated current events.

GIRL: I do. But that's not the same as the world. That just shows the limitations of your thinking. You've never been particularly deep.

BOY: Why did you marry me then?

GIRL: I thought you'd get better.

BOY: Better? You thought I was a fixer-upper.

GIRL: You could put it like that, yes.

BOY: Well, did I?

GIRL: Did you what?

BOY: Did I get better?

GIRL: No, you just got *fatter*. You started eating those

chocolates and you never stopped and you just got—immense.

BOY: I'm not all that fat.

GIRL: Oh yes, you are. You are also a living *dis*proof of the old adage that fat people are jolly. You are dull dull dull. *(She reaches for the chocolate.)*

BOY: Dull am I. Give me that piece of chocolate.

GIRL: No, you said it was mine.

BOY: But you don't need it. You're getting fat.

GIRL: You're fatter than I am.

BOY: I tell you what: let's give the chocolate to charity. We'll go outside and hand it with our compliments to the first kid we see.

GIRL: He won't take it. Kids aren't supposed to take candy from strangers.

BOY: We'll introduce ourselves.

GIRL: We're still strangers. Besides, if he took it, it would be setting a bad precedent. Someone might want to give him poison candy.

BOY: Maybe I'm trying to give *you* poison candy.

GIRL: You haven't the imagination.

BOY: Oh, I haven't, eh. I tell you, I've been reading a lot of books lately.

GIRL: This is, I'm sure, a recent development.

BOY: And they have a lot of ideas about handling people like you.

GIRL: What books?

BOY: Well, *Mein Kampf* by Hitler.

GIRL: You've been reading *Mein Kampf*?

BOY: Yes, and he has a few ideas I'd like to try out. You know, Western women have too much freedom. Nietzsche said, "Truth is a woman. That's why she loves a soldier."

GIRL: Nietzsche ended up in the nut house. Which, I might add, is where you're likely to wind up too.

BOY: Listen, I'm serious.

GIRL: You couldn't be serious if you grew two heads.

BOY: And you are, huh?

GIRL: I have my serious side, yes. That doesn't mean I'm against fun.

BOY: And what do you think of as fun?

GIRL: *Eating chocolates. (She gulps the chocolate down.)*

BOY: You ate the chocolate.

GIRL: I did.

BOY: It was the last piece.

GIRL: It was.

EPILOGUE: TWO PLAYS

BOY: I thought you'd give the chocolate to me.

GIRL: You offered it to me. I ate it.

BOY: I thought if I mentioned you were putting on weight you'd hand it back to me. And then I could eat it.

GIRL: You offered it to me hoping I'd give it back to you?

BOY: Well, yes. That sometimes happens.

GIRL: Not in this case. Yum yum it was delicious.

BOY: That was the last chocolate.

GIRL: The last.

BOY: I'll never buy you another box of chocolates.

GIRL: You didn't. I bought this box. It's *my* box.

BOY: Well, you can have it.

GIRL: I did.

BOY: Bitch.

GIRL: Bastard.

(Long silence)

BOY: What's on television?

GIRL: Nothing but reruns.

BOY: Wanna go out?

GIRL: No.

(Long silence)

BOY: Hey, honey. Let's make up.

GIRL: Why?

(Long silence)

BOY: I have another box of chocolates.

GIRL: Where?

BOY: I hid it in the closet.

GIRL *(Excitedly but happily)*: That's *terrible!*

BOY: Let's go eat them all.

GIRL: Let's get fat.

BOY: First, can I read you my poem?

GIRL: All right. What is it?

BOY: It's called "The Skeleton's Defense of Carnality."

(Recites. Note: He recites the poem as a professional poet would; as poet he is no longer the character we have been watching.)

> Truly I have lost weight, I *have*
> lost weight,
> grown lean in love's defense,
> in love's defense grown grave.
> It was concupiscence
> that brought me to the state:
> all bone and a bit of skin
> to keep the bone within.
> Flesh is no heavy burden

EPILOGUE: TWO PLAYS

>for one possessed of little
>and accustomed to its loss.
>I lean to love, which leaves me lean
>till lean turn into lack.
>A wanton bone, I sing my song
>and travel where the bone is blown
>and extricate true love from lust
>as any man of wisdom must.
>Then wherefore should I rage
>against this pilgrimage
>from gravel unto gravel?
>Circuitous I travel
>from love to lack
>and lack to lack,
>from lean to lack
>and back.

(Brief silence)

GIRL: What a strange poem. I have a poem, too.

(Recites)

>Who do we fall
>in love with if not
>ourselves?—starstruck, stupid
>are what we feel when "struck" by Cupid
>"Falling in love" is what
>we have instead of God

The powerful need for self-abasement
leads to our own effacement
"To thy high requiem become a sod"
wrote Keats, who understood
these things too well, and Anne Francis
in this film, fearful and beautiful, is a statue, a woman turned to wood
I think of Chet Baker with his thin voice and
    marvelous horn:
the sudden presence of heroin

(As GIRL recites the last line, she mimes injecting a needle into her veins; then she opens her arms to the world.)

(She is still.)

BOY *(Indicating her, admiringly, spelling it slowly)*: Heroine! H—e—r—o—i—n—e.

Tableau and

END

SHAVIUS / DIABOLUS

a ten-minute play

A tall, thin old man with bushy eyebrows and white hair arrives in Hell, which is not "a city much like Seville" but merely an empty stage. A wisp of smoke blows by. The man pinches his arm.

EPILOGUE: TWO PLAYS

Am I really here. Alive? Or is this some last dream before I'm thrown on the scrap heap?

A man appears at the side of the stage. He is dressed impeccably in a fashionable suit and tie. He has the merest hint of horns on his forehead to tell us who he is.

This *is* the scrap heap, Mr. Shaw. But welcome, I have enjoyed reading your works. They are quite popular here in Hell. *(Brief flash of lights, suggesting hellfire.)*

GEORGE BERNARD SHAW *(amused)*: Well, I have definitely been called a devil. But you, sir, are, I take it, *(indicating the horns on the man's head)* the very thing itself.

DEVIL: Only a minor functionary, I assure you. These horns (far more useful than the angelic halo, don't you think?) are a recent acquisition—the result of a promotion. I am merely your welcoming committee.

SHAW: Most kind.

DEVIL: Not at all. As you pointed out in *Man and Superman*, since we are no longer limited to the body, we can appear in any way we wish. You for example might appear as a strong and healthy version of yourself—say, at forty-five. A vital man.

Suddenly Shaw is forty-five years old. Red-bearded, erect.

DEVIL: You see, well-done!

SHAW *(pleased)*: We dramatists are accustomed to dealing with illusion.

DEVIL: As are the fallen angels. One might say that illusion is the only way we can bear reality—so there is nothing but illusion here. We are all on a bare stage with no scenery except for what we can create from our imaginations. Would you care for Brazil?

SHAW: No, thank you. A bare stage suits me. I will tell you should I have any further requirements. What is to be done with me?

DEVIL: You are to be judged.

SHAW: I have always had the suspicion that critics were secretly devils and devils critics.

DEVIL: We would not dream of judging your work. It is your soul in which we are interested.

SHAW: Quite an appendage, the soul. So I have one, do I?

DEVIL: We believe so. But so much of our lives is illusion it is difficult to tell.

SHAW: And who is my judge to be?

DEVIL: *Him*—or perhaps it is *Her*. *(Flash of lights again.)*

SHAW: You don't know?

DEVIL: No. We are in darkness here. "No light but rather darkness visible," as your English poet put it.

SHAW: What are you planning to do with me?

DEVIL: I—or, I should say, we—have no plans. We have summoned you to this empty stage. And we have given

EPILOGUE: TWO PLAYS

you a character: me. What will you do with it?

SHAW: I could fill your mouth with speeches.

DEVIL: As indeed you did very well. But I am a problem as a character. I don't know who I am. And you don't know either.

SHAW: I can give you an identity. You are—Adam the gardener!

DEVIL: But that is only your illusion, not mine. I know nothing of flowers or plants. But I have seen *you* in your secret moments. I have seen you when you most despaired. Do you remember? I am no gardener, but I felt such sorrow for you that day when I saw you weeping in the garden...Or was that someone else?

SHAW: It was, I believe, a man far greater than I. A religious fanatic, but a genius. He was of course destroyed for his activities, which he was unable to disguise as playwriting. He was then resurrected—a pure fiction—and the image of the crime against him became the centerpiece of a monstrous body of thought which destroyed thousands.

DEVIL: Christianity, you mean. Yes, we dislike it here as well. Many of our finest people have adopted the stance of atheism.

SHAW: I was no atheist but a believer in the Life Force.

DEVIL: Perhaps the greatest illusion of all. As if life had to have a purpose.

SHAW: It has *one* purpose: to achieve consciousness of itself. Exactly what you say you lack.

DEVIL: Yes, it's true. I may have some awareness of you, but little of myself. None of my self. Perhaps I have no self.

SHAW: Then you are a dramatist! I should have known that the devil who would greet me would have been a playwright.

DEVIL: Yes, I believe that's right. Yes, I *was* a playwright. Something is coming back to me now. I remember: *To be or not to be...* But that is as far as I can reach.

SHAW: It is my particular hell to meet William Shakespeare! You, sir, have been my father and my great example and my great antagonist—though you were of course unaware of it. It is an honor to meet you.

DEVIL: No, I am only a minor functionary. Not a top dog. Only a bottom.

SHAW: Yes, Bottom. That was one of your characters.

DEVIL: And an ass.

SHAW: Yes, Bottom became an ass. You don't remember?

DEVIL: No, I'm afraid not. When I died, my soul went out of me and left me only this shell of substance which you see before you. You too will begin to forget. It will be a great blessing but a source of embarrassment when you encounter those who still have memory. Those like yourself.

EPILOGUE: TWO PLAYS

SHAW: Yes, I remember it all—the whole glorious, mistaken thing I called "my life." What a time!

DEVIL: But this is not time at all. This is eternity. It will be a long winter's nap.

SHAW: The devil!

DEVIL: You are trying to deny it, but things are already beginning to go, aren't they. You are beginning to forget who you were—because you are no longer that. Time is only real here for that moment of forgetting. Then it vanishes entirely.

SHAW: But I thought I was to be judged.

DEVIL: (*suddenly realizing, smiling at the realization*) This *is* your judgment. It is the judgment of the most high that you are to forget. The very thing you valued—consciousness—will be taken from you. Look, there are the lights again. (*Flash of lights*)

SHAW: I can't imagine that.

DEVIL: You were nothing more than a shell the Life Force filled. Now, it has moved on. Even the stage we stand on will be vanishing.

SHAW: Yes, I remember your saying such things in your plays.

DEVIL: Plays? Plays are nothing. You and I stand on the edge of an abyss. (*Gesturing towards the audience.*) Whatever audience we have is as much in motion as we. We have been men, but now... The Life Force has amused itself with us, and now it has abandoned us. We are vanishing, vanishing.

(The lights begin to dim.)

We are such stuff as dreams are made on.

SHAW *(putting his hand to his ear)*: What do you say? Dreams?

DEVIL: Not even dreams.

SHAW: Drams?

DEVIL: Not even drams. Nor trams. Nor

(The light grows fainter and fainter)

SHAW *(reciting from* Man and Superman*)*: "You think that you are Ann's suitor; that you are the pursuer and she the pursued; that it is your part to woo, to persuade, to prevail, to overcome. Fool: it is you who are the pursued, the marked down quarry, the destined prey. You need not sit looking longingly at the bait through the wires of the trap: the door is open, and will remain so until it shuts behind you forever."

DEVIL: "Behind you forever."

SHAW: To wait in the dark

DEVIL: *a deep moan*

SHAW: for a day of steam and wet

EPILOGUE: TWO PLAYS

DEVIL: *cutting through everything*

SHAW: life as it should be

DEVIL: *to a fierce dark ecstasy*

The light slowly vanishes as the two men begin to speak a chorus. Their voices alternate at each line at first, then, when that is concluded, each speaks the entire passage all the way through. One begins, "the yellowish pallor moves: there is an old crone wandering in the void"; when that is finished, the second begins, "the yellowish pallor moves: there is an old crone wandering in the void." The line, "it is our only refuge from heaven" receives particular emphasis by both speakers. As they finish, the light is gone entirely.

the yellowish pallor moves: there is an old crone wandering in the void

I have wandered for hours in horrible loneliness   that's understood isn't it   branded with her shame   barren, the Life Force passes it by   who would like to be a better man   our minds are nothing but this knowledge of ourselves   treat us well: we will not prove ungrateful
   Go to the bee, thou poet   that is not happiness but the price for which the strong sell their happiness   I remember: he came to heaven   beware of the man whose god is in the skies   the mere transfiguration of institutions   I should laugh at you, Jack   vital economy is the philosopher's stone   she habitually and unscrupulously uses her personal fascination to make men give her whatever she wants   from the darkness   of the dark-

ness   to the darkness   the lifelong imprisonment of penniless men

and when a negro is dipped in kerosene and set on fire in America at the present time   crowds of respectable, charitable, virtuously indignant, high-minded citizens   the things our moral monsters do may be left out of account   the horror of the one the loneliness of the other   compulsory   chattel   labor   a horse may live from 24 to 40 years   I am thinking of my dear mother when I think of you   of the darkness

matrimonomaniacs!   evolving today a mind's eye that shall see, not the physical world but the purpose of life   from the darkness   to   hell is the home of the unreal and of the seekers for happiness   *it is the only refuge from heaven*   darkness

Acknowledgements

The author wishes to thank the editors of the magazines in which some of these pieces appeared.

"Sous le Pont Mirbeau" was published in the print/online magazine, *Caveat Lector*.

"Broughton Fountain" appeared in *Exquisite Corpse*.

"Bus Ride" and "The Tiger" appeared in my book, *Adrift* (1993).

"The Old Man" appeared in *2 Bridges Review* and in my book, *EYES* (2013).

"My Death," "The Ern Malley Story" and "Malèna" also appeared in *EYES*.

"Man Wolf" (which is in free verse) appeared in my book, *RIVERRUN* (2016).

Both *The Boy, the Girl, and the Piece of Chocolate* and *Shavius / Diabolus* have been performed. California productions were directed by Lewis Campbell. The New York production of *The Boy, the Girl, and the Piece of Chocolate* was directed by Barbara Bosch. The play was also made into a film by Alabama filmmaker Wayne Sides.

Photo by Robert Schneck (1987)

Jack Foley (born 1940) has published thirteen books of poetry, five books of criticism, and *Visions and Affiliations*, a "chronoencyclopedia" of California poetry from 1940 to 2005.

His radio show, *Cover to Cover*, is heard on Berkeley station KPFA every Wednesday at 3; his column, "Foley's Books," appears in the online magazine, *The Alsop Review*.

With his late wife, Adelle, Foley performed his work (often "multivoiced" pieces) frequently in the San Francisco Bay Area. He is continuing to work with others. With poet Clara Hsu, Foley is co-publisher of Poetry Hotel Press.

In 2010 Foley was awarded the Lifetime Achievement Award by the Berkeley Poetry Festival, and June 5, 2010 was proclaimed "Jack Foley Day" in Berkeley.